Cruise, Beth.
Silver spurs

SILVER SPURS

D1125764

"Saved by the Bell" titles include:

Mark-Paul Gosselaar: Ultimate Gold
Mario Lopez: High-Voltage Star
Behind the Scenes at "Saved by the Bell"
Beauty and Fitness with "Saved by the Bell"
Dustin Diamond: Teen Star
The "Saved by the Bell" Date Book

Hot fiction titles:

SILVER SPURS

by Beth Cruise

St. Benedict School
220 N. 7th St.
Cambridge, Ohio 43725

Collier Books
Macmillan Publishing Company
New York
Maxwell Macmillan Canada
Toronto
Maxwell Macmillan International
New York   Oxford   Singapore   Sydney

Photograph and logo copyright © 1994 by National Broadcasting
Company, Inc. All rights reserved. "Saved by the Bell"™ is a trademark of
the National Broadcasting Company, Inc. Used under license.
Text copyright © 1994 by Collier Books, Macmillan Publishing Company
All rights reserved. No part of this book may be reproduced or transmitted
in any form or by any means, electronic or mechanical, including photo-
copying, recording, or by any information storage and retrieval system,
without permission in writing from the Publisher.

Collier Books
Macmillan Publishing Company
866 Third Avenue
New York, NY 10022
Maxwell Macmillan Canada, Inc.
1200 Eglinton Avenue East
Suite 200
Don Mills, Ontario M3C 3N1
Macmillan Publishing Company is part of the Maxwell Communication
Group of Companies.
First Collier Books edition 1994
Printed in the United States of America
10 9 8 7 6 5 4 3 2 1

Library of Congress Cataloging-in-Publication Data
Cruise, Beth.
Silver spurs / by Beth Cruise. – 1st Collier Books ed.
p.   cm.
Summary: The "Saved by the Bell" gang heads out to a New Mexican
dude ranch for a weekend of fun that is soon complicated by Zack's being
mistaken for a rodeo star and Jessie's suspicions of the ranch owner's past.
ISBN 0-02-042788-3
[1. Ranch life–New Mexico–Fiction. 2. New Mexico–Fiction.] I. Title.
PZ7.C88827Si 1994
[Fic]–dc20   94-6552

To
all the
"Saved by the Bell"
cowboys and cowgirls

Chapter 1

▼ ▲ ▼ ▲ ▼

Zack Morris dropped his books onto his favorite table at his favorite hangout, the Max. He surveyed his four friends, who were sleepily eating their various breakfasts.

"You have to save me!" he cried dramatically.

Kelly Kapowski, his girlfriend, looked up from her glass of juice. "Please, Zack," she moaned, stifling a yawn. "Even *you* can't be in trouble this early. It's not even eight o'clock yet."

"I'm not even awake," A. C. Slater grumbled from behind his sunglasses. He took a sip of coffee.

"Save you from what, Zack?" Samuel "Screech" Powers asked as he spread jelly over the cream cheese on his bagel. He leaned down to inspect his handiwork and got cream cheese on his nose. A clump attached itself to a stray frizzy curl.

Lisa Turtle shuddered. "Why do I come here in the mornings?" she asked, directing the question to the air.

"Because that way I'm the first thing you see," Screech said, batting his stubby eyelashes at her. Despite Lisa's complete lack of interest in him, Screech was convinced that they shared a romantic destiny.

"*Thing* is right." Lisa handed him a napkin. "I'd rather smooch it up with your pet salamander, Screech."

"Would you, Lisa?" Screech beamed. "I have Algernon right here in my pocket."

"Ewwww," Lisa moaned, sliding closer to the wall. Lisa was a completely feminine girl, right down to her salmon-colored nails. She considered long-lash mascara a staple of any household, along with bread and milk.

"Let's get back to poor Morris here," Slater said. "He wants us to save him, remember?"

"That's right, Zack," Kelly said, her deep blue eyes amused. "Who do we have to save you from this time? Mr. Belding? Did you cut class again?"

Mr. Belding was the principal of Bayside High. He and Zack had a deep, meaningful relationship that revolved around detention.

"No, wait," Slater said with his trademark smirk. "Let me guess. It's your dad again. You catered another gourmet lunch for your entire French class on his account at Chez Louis. And you didn't even get extra credit."

"No, guys," Zack said. "It's none of those things. I wish it was one of those things, but it's not. I want you to save me from myself."

"From yourself?" Kelly asked, puzzled.

"Wait, I get it," Lisa said. "You're about to get yourself in trouble, right?"

"No!" Zack cried. "That's just it, Lisa! I'm *not* in trouble, I wasn't *just* in trouble yesterday, and I won't *be* in trouble tomorrow!"

"Isn't that good?" Kelly asked, confused.

"It might be good," Zack said mournfully. "But it's boring. Don't you feel it, guys?" he asked, looking around the table at his friends. "It's the middle of the week in the middle of the month in the middle of the semester in the middle of the year. Times aren't great. They aren't awful. They're . . . normal!" Zack gave a deep shudder.

Kelly laughed. "That's just your trouble, Zack. You think normal is boring. I happen to like normal."

"Me, too," Screech said.

"Screech, you wouldn't know normal if it came up and bit you on the nose," Lisa said. "And if it did come up and bite you on the nose, it would get a mouthful of cream cheese." She handed him another napkin.

"I agree with Kelly," Slater said. "What's wrong with normal? It's eighty degrees out and sunny. After school, I'm going to hit the beach. Maybe play a little tennis with Jessie. Have a taco and head on home for an evening of studying and channel surfing. Tomorrow I'll wake up and do it all over again. If you ask me, normal in Palisades, California, is pretty close to paradise."

"Yeah," Kelly said, nodding.

"If the forecast for the rest of my life was sunny and warm, I'd want to jump off a cliff," Zack said. "Where are the storms? Where's the danger? Where's the beef?"

"Zack, I don't think the Max will serve you a hamburger at breakfast," Screech said thoughtfully. "You could get a side order of bacon, though."

"Zack, exciting things happen all the time," Kelly protested. She held up her glass of juice. "The Max put in a juice bar this week, didn't they? I got papaya this morning."

Zack looked tenderly at his gorgeous girl-friend. She was the best person he'd ever met, as well as the nicest. But sometimes he wondered if she got up every morning and took a happy pill.

Nobody could be as cheerful as Kelly and still be human.

"That's nice, Kelly," he said, patting her hand.

"Tomorrow I'm going to try raspberry-banana," Kelly said happily.

"Wow," Zack said. "I'm happy for you, Kelly. But if something doesn't happen to shake things up around here, I'm going to burst!"

"Maybe on Friday they'll have mango-pineapple," Screech said consolingly.

"I've got something even better," a teasing voice said.

The gang had been so caught up in their conversation that they hadn't noticed that Jessie Spano was standing beside the booth. Her backpack was slung over one shoulder and her hazel eyes were sparkling. She tossed her long, curly brown hair over her shoulder and slid into the booth next to Slater.

"What's better than mango-pineapple juice?" Screech asked.

"Love," Jessie said.

"That's for sure," Lisa sighed.

"I agree," Slater said. "Love is not, however, better than tacos."

Jessie grinned at him. "I'll see how you feel about that on the beach Saturday night."

"Whoa, momma," Slater teased back. "Just don't forget the guacamole, so we can make it a real contest."

Jessie gave Slater a punch on the arm. At least it was just a tap. Now that they were dating again, the gang was always ready for Jessie to slug him. Jessie and Slater were just as likely to fight as they were to kiss.

"So who are you in love with, Jessie?" Lisa asked with a grin. "It can't be with that caveman sitting next to you."

Slater flexed a muscular arm. "Hey, I'm not a caveman. I'm an athlete in top shape who happens to believe that women should be protected and men are the ones to do it."

"You see what I mean?" Lisa sighed.

Jessie grinned. "I'm not talking about me. I'm talking about my mother. She's head over heels in love with a fantastic guy. He's so romantic. He just sent her two dozen long-stem yellow roses."

"Wow," Kelly breathed.

"Gee," Lisa sighed.

"You see, Zack?" Kelly said. "Exciting things do happen in Palisades."

"Be still, my beating heart," Zack said. "Jessie's mother has a new boyfriend. I must have missed the headline in this morning's paper."

"Come on, Jessie," Kelly said, leaning forward and ignoring Zack. "Spill it."

"Details, girlfriend," Lisa ordered.

"His name is Chance Gifford," Jessie said. "He's a cowboy!"

"Well, git along, little dogies," Slater said sarcastically.

"I mean a *modern* cowboy," Jessie said, her hazel eyes shining. "He owns this fabulous dude ranch and resort right outside of Santa Fe, New Mexico. Mom has been dating him for about six months, whenever he's in Palisades. I haven't actually met him yet, since I spend weekends with my dad. But the way my mom talks about him, I think they might get married! Isn't that great?"

"Whoa, wait a second here," Zack said. "Is this Jessie Spano talking? The girl who went ballistic when her father got remarried?"

"I admit I had a hard time when Dad decided to marry Leslie," Jessie said. "I still kind of hoped that my parents would get back together. But I'm more mature now."

"Do you really think they'll get married?" Kelly asked.

Jessie nodded. "I think it's definitely a possibility."

"But what will happen to you?" Lisa asked. "You can't move away from Palisades!"

"Of course not," Jessie said. "My mom told me that *if* they decide to get married, she wouldn't move until I graduated. After that I'd be going away to school, anyway. And Mom said that if she moved to Santa Fe, she'd still want to keep our house in Palisades. She'd miss the coast too much if she sold it. Just think," Jessie said, her expression faraway. "It would be so perfect. Santa Fe is supposed to be beautiful. I'd get to visit this luxurious spa and ranch on my vacations. And we'd still have the house here!"

"It sounds perfect," Lisa said with a sigh. "You could have a pedicure every day."

"It sounds incredibly romantic to me," Kelly breathed. "Finding true love at last."

"When Mom told me, I started to cry," Jessie confided. "She's so happy. She *glows*. It's all so perfect."

Zack sniffed loudly. "I'm so touched. Cowboy love stories always make me cry. Slater, can I borrow your handkerchief?" he asked, dabbing at his eyes.

"As soon as I finish wringing it out," Slater said. He pretended to wipe his eyes with his napkin. "I've never been so moved in my life."

"Did you ever hear the one about Roy Rogers

and Trigger?" Zack said, faking a sob. "Now, *that* was a romance."

Tears were rolling down Screech's face. "That one always gets me, too," he blubbered.

"Don't you guys have any heart?" Kelly said to Zack and Slater.

"Aren't you happy for Mrs. Spano?" Lisa added, frowning.

"Of course I am," Zack said. "But not to be self-centered or anything, what does this have to do with me?"

"We'd *never* call you self-centered, Zack," Lisa said, rolling her eyes.

"Actually, Zack, you might be interested in what came with the box of roses," Jessie said.

"Now, don't tell me," Zack said. "Chocolate spurs?"

Jessie shook her head. "Chance has invited me and my mom up to the Lazybones Ranch over the three-day weekend coming up. And he said I could bring as many of my friends as I wanted."

"Great," Zack said. "It's easy for him to invite us when he knows we can't possibly go. The airfare must be super expensive."

"That's the best part," Jessie said. "Chance is a pilot, and he has his own private plane. He's offered to fly down and pick us up on Friday and then fly us back home late Monday afternoon!"

The gang exchanged dumbfounded glances. A free vacation in New Mexico! This was the best news they'd heard in weeks!

"How's that for excitement, Morris?" Jessie smirked.

"Slater, can I have that hankie?" Zack asked. "I think I *am* going to cry!"

Chapter 2

▼ ▲ ▼ ▲ ▼

Friday was just a couple of days away, but for Jessie, it seemed to take forever to arrive. She wished she could spend the time doing something: for instance, packing and repacking her suitcase, like Lisa. Or searching every store in Palisades for a pair of chaps, like Screech. But she couldn't. All she could do was worry and dream.

Worry: Would Slater finally come to his senses and realize that she was the only girl for him?

Dream: The magic and beauty of the high desert of New Mexico would inspire Slater. One night, under a canopy of stars, he would ask her to go steady.

Jessie and Slater's romance had always been filled with ups and downs. In fact, it was a regular

220 N. 7th St.
Cambridge, Ohio 43725

roller coaster. But now Jessie felt that at last they were ready to handle the responsibilities of a committed relationship. One that wouldn't be filled with games and jealousy. It would be solid. Mature.

Besides, if she had to spend one more Saturday night wondering what Slater was doing and who he was doing it with, she'd have no fingernails left.

▲   ▼   ▲

The big day finally arrived. The gang had only a half day of school on Friday, so they'd brought their gear with them. Jessie's mother was picking them up there to drive them to the airport. Everyone had crammed what they could into small weekend bags. It was lucky the rest of the gang had packed light, since Lisa had brought three suitcases.

"Lisa, Chance asked us to pack light," Jessie said.

"I did!" Lisa exclaimed.

"This is *light*?" Slater asked, looking at Lisa's set of matching luggage.

"I didn't pack my curling iron," Lisa said defensively. "Or my facial sauna. I just pray my pores don't get clogged."

Just then Mrs. Spano pulled up. "Hey, gang!" she called cheerfully. "Are you ready for an adventure?" She got out of the car to open the trunk. Mrs. Spano was a tall, willowy woman with a lighter version of Jessie's hazel eyes.

"Gosh, Mrs. Spano, I almost didn't recognize you without your briefcase," Zack teased. He'd lived next door to the Spanos for ages and considered Mrs. Spano his second mom. She was a dedicated public defender, and she usually greeted Zack at the door carrying an armload of files and a briefcase stuffed with papers.

"And, look, no suit," Mrs. Spano said with a grin. "Blue jeans. It's the new me." She pirouetted for Zack, showing him her casual outfit of jeans and cowboy boots.

Zack gave a short whistle. "Wow. You look almost young, Mrs. Spano."

"Gee, thanks, Zack," Jessie's mom said. "I think."

Zack, Slater, Kelly, Lisa, and Jessie loaded their bags into the back of Mrs. Spano's car.

"Next stop, the Wild West," Slater said.

"Wait a sec," Kelly said. "Where's Screech?"

Suddenly, the double front doors of Bayside High crashed open. Screech stood in the doorway dressed in chaps, a fringed vest, and a ten-gallon cowboy hat.

"Howdy, pardners," he called. "Let's go rustle up some dogies."

Lisa rolled her eyes. "Kelly, did you have to remember him?" she asked with a groan.

▲   ▼   ▲

When they reached the special hangar for private planes, they saw a tall, well-built man in jeans and a flight jacket leaning against the building. When he saw them, he flashed a devastating grin.

"Wow," Lisa breathed.

"Gosh," Jessie said.

"He's gorgeous," Kelly murmured as Mrs. Spano ran forward. Chance picked her up and gave her a big kiss.

"I'll say he's gorgeous, girlfriend," Lisa said. "He makes Mel Gibson look like Huckleberry Hound."

"I can't really tell from here, but I bet his hairline is receding," Zack said.

"He's not as tall as he looks, either," Slater observed. "He's wearing cowboy boots."

"He's flying you to Santa Fe for free and putting you up in a luxurious resort," Jessie reminded them in a deceptively sweet tone. "Or maybe you'd like to stay home for the three-day weekend?"

"What a handsome guy," Zack said quickly.

"He looks real smart, too," Slater agreed.

Chance strode over to them. He went right up

to Jessie. "You've got to be Kate's daughter," he said. "You're just as beautiful as your mother."

Jessie blushed and shook Chance's hand. "I want to introduce you to my friends," she said.

One by one, Chance met the gang and shook each of their hands.

"Thank you so much for having us, Mr. Gifford," Lisa said.

"It's my pleasure, Lisa," he said. "But call me Chance. I've checked the weather patterns and it looks like we'll have a smooth flight. It's clear, so you'll have a great bird's-eye view of the most beautiful country you've ever seen. New Mexico is called the Land of Enchantment, and you can really see why from the air."

"We're looking forward to it," Mrs. Spano said.

"Then let's get started," Chance said. "We'll be in Santa Fe in time for an early dinner. I made a reservation at my favorite restaurant in town."

Chance tucked one of Lisa's suitcases underneath his arm and picked up the other two without even a grunt. He strode toward the small plane waiting on the runway.

"Wow," Lisa said, impressed. "Now, there's a man for you. Anybody who can carry all my suitcases gets my vote."

"What he'll probably get is a hernia," Zack observed.

▲   ▼   ▲

Chance was right. The flight was incredible. As they crossed the border into New Mexico, below them were beautiful purple mountains, deep canyons, and long stretches of golden desert dotted with sage.

"Santa Fe is what is called high desert," Chance explained. "We're at a high elevation here, so the vegetation is quite different from what you're used to in California."

"It's beautiful," Kelly said, her nose pressed to the window.

"Look," Jessie said as the plane dipped lower in the sky. "Yucca."

"Jessie, you shouldn't insult the landscape," Screech whispered. "It's Chance's home."

Jessie laughed. "Yucca is a plant, Screech. See the yellow flowers?"

"Here we are, gang," Chance called out as they swooped over the airport. In another minute, they were landing on the runway as though it were a cloud. Could Chance Gifford do everything well? Jessie wondered. He sure seemed like the perfect man. And he could even be the perfect stepfather.

They all piled into Chance's Jeep Cherokee for the ride into Santa Fe. "You guys can explore town after dinner," he told them as he navigated the narrow streets around the large plaza in the center of town. "I have a feeling we're all pretty hungry. I got a table overlooking the plaza so you can get a taste of the town along with your dinner."

Chance led the way up a flight of outdoor stairs to a restaurant on the second level of a building. It had large windows overlooking the grassy plaza. Everyone gathered around a long pine table.

Chance explained some of the unfamiliar items on the menu. He knew the name of every pepper and what went into every sauce, and he helped each of them order while they munched on chips and delicious salsa. Steaming platters of food soon arrived, and the gang ate one of the most delicious meals of their lives.

"Oof," Jessie said when it was over. "I'm stuffed."

"Those were the best enchiladas I've ever had," Kelly said. "Now that I know what a chipolte pepper is, I'm going to order it again."

"I never knew there were so many different kinds of chili peppers," Slater added.

"Is there a fire extinguisher around here, Chance?" Zack asked, fanning himself. "I might need it to cool down my mouth."

"Honey, you'd need a whole fire department to cool down that big mouth of yours," Lisa said, and everyone laughed.

"I'm used to spicy food," Chance said. "But if you kids need cooling down, there's an ice-cream shop down the block."

"Ice cream!" Screech said. "I hope they don't put jalapeños in that, too."

"Why don't you kids wander around and explore while Chance and I have our coffee?" Mrs. Spano suggested. "We can meet at the car in an hour."

"We'll have a pretty ride to the ranch. The sun will be setting over the mountains," Chance said.

Everyone agreed it was a perfect plan. But once they got out on the street, no one could agree on what to do. Zack and Screech wanted to get ice cream. Kelly and Lisa wanted to look at silver jewelry, and Slater wanted to look at Native American pottery. Jessie wanted to sit on a bench on the square and absorb the atmosphere. Besides, she felt too full to move.

They finally decided that the only solution was to split up. Jessie headed for the square. After only a short time sitting still while the sun slid lower in the sky, Jessie was convinced that Santa Fe was the most magical city she'd ever seen. She loved the low adobe buildings and the colorful wares in the shops.

She'd only been here a few hours, but already Jessie felt at home in Santa Fe. And she hadn't even seen Chance's ranch yet. This could be a whole new life for her mom *and* for her, Jessie thought happily. The thought of spending more time in Santa Fe was totally thrilling.

Jessie watched as her mom and Chance exited the restaurant, hand in hand. She didn't think she'd ever seen her mom look so happy. And she hadn't realized how pretty she still was.

The pair turned down a side street, and Jessie got up to follow them. She crossed the square and turned the corner just in time to see her mom touch Chance's arm and gesture toward an art gallery. Chance nodded, and Mrs. Spano pushed the door open and went inside. Chance ambled next door and bought a newspaper. He stood on the sidewalk, scanning the headlines.

Jessie hurried across the street. She was glad Chance was alone. It would give her an opportunity to talk to him in private. She really wanted to get to know him.

His back to her, Chance began to fold the paper and start toward the art gallery. Jessie was just about to say his name when she heard a woman call "Chuck!"

Chance stopped for only a split second and then kept on walking.

"Chuck MacGuffin!"

An older woman dressed in a sweatshirt with a

coyote on the front approached Chance. Jessie hung back, but she could hear the woman clearly.

"I'd have known you anywhere," the woman said. "Chuck, how are you? How long has it been? Seven years? No, eight, I think. Land sakes, you're a sight for sore eyes."

Chance looked the woman straight in the eye. "I'm sorry, ma'am," he said pleasantly. "But I'm afraid you've mistaken me for someone else. My name's not Chuck MacGuffin."

The woman stared at him. "But—"

He tipped his cowboy hat. "You have a good evening now," he said. He turned and walked into the gallery. The woman stood for a minute, watching him. Then she walked away, shaking her head.

Jessie frowned. That was weird. Chance must be almost a double for this guy Chuck, because the woman seemed positive she was right, even when Chance was only inches away from her face.

Jessie shrugged away what she'd seen. It must have been a case of mistaken identity, she told herself. It happened all the time. Besides, Chance was way too cool and this place was way too fabulous for anything strange to be going on.

Chapter 3

▼　▲　▼　▲　▼

Zack reached for a black cowboy hat and plopped it down on his head. He turned around to show Screech.

"How do I look?"

"Awesome," Screech said. "But I'm telling you right now. You can't have my chaps."

Zack turned to contemplate himself in the mirror of the store selling western clothing. His hazel eyes glinted from underneath the brim. He tilted the hat at a dashing angle and flashed a cocky smile. He thought he looked pretty awesome, too.

Suddenly someone clapped him on the back and he shot forward, bumping against the mirror. Annoyed, Zack turned around and saw a big, beefy guy with a huge grin on his face.

"You're the greatest, pal!" the guy said.

"Uh, thanks," Zack replied. He turned back to adjust the tilt of the hat. In the mirror, he saw a middle-aged woman wink at him and wave. He waved back.

He turned to examine a display of bandannas. A guy picking out a yellow one gave him a thumbs-up sign. "Good luck to you!" he called.

"Boy," Zack said, sidling over to Screech. "Santa Fe sure is a friendly town."

Across the store, a trio of three pretty girls who were trying on cowboy boots pointed at him. Then they waved and giggled.

"Maybe it's the hat," Zack mused.

"Can I borrow it?" Screech asked. "Maybe it would work on Lisa."

A man in a checked shirt heading for the counter stopped when he saw Zack.

"How's it going, Dave?" he asked Zack.

Zack looked behind him. "Huh? Me?"

The guy winked at him. "Traveling incognito, huh?"

"No," Zack said. "I'm just not Dave."

The guy nodded. "Riiiiight," he said, winking again. "I'll leave you alone then."

"Did you hear that?" Zack said to Screech as the guy walked away. "I must look like some guy named Dave."

"Daredevil Dave!" A tall, skinny man approached him. "I caught you in Wichita last summer. I'd like to shake your hand."

"Who do you think I am?" Zack asked.

"Shucks, I *know* who you are," the man replied. "You're Daredevil Dave Laramie, the best rodeo performer in the West." He elbowed Zack. "Not that you'd get much competition from the dudes back East."

"We have dudes in California, too," Screech piped up. "They hang out at the beach and surf, mostly. 'Hey, dude, rilly awesome set out there today,'" he continued, demonstrating California dude-speak.

The man gave him a short, puzzled look and turned back to Zack. "Anyway, you've got more guts in your little toe than most men have in their . . . uh, whole feet."

"Gee, thanks," Zack said. "But I'm not who you think I am."

"Suuure," the man said. "I get it, Daredevil."

"How'd you know?" Screech asked. "My friend really *is* known as a daredevil back home. Especially when it comes to cutting classes. And once he piled seventeen lawn chairs on top of each other and dived into Nanny Parker's pool."

The man looked at Screech as though he were a strange variety of mushroom he didn't want to try. Then he returned his attention to Zack. "Good luck, Dave."

"Wait," Zack said, but the man was already walking away. He turned to Screech. "Screech, we have to do something. Everybody thinks I'm this Daredevil Dave guy."

"Who?" Screech asked.

"Daredevil Dave!"

"Never heard of him," Screech said, shaking his head.

"I haven't, either! Screech, listen to me. I must look like this guy Dave. He's some big rodeo performer. We should tell people that I'm not him or I could wind up on some bucking bronco!"

"At least you have the right hat," Screech observed.

"Screech!"

"Okay, okay!" Screech said, holding up a hand. "I'll loan you my chaps."

Zack closed his eyes in thought. "Screech, this could definitely make for a very interesting weekend."

When he opened his eyes, the three girls who had been trying on cowboy boots were standing in front of him, smiling.

Zack instantly zeroed in on the tall girl with light green eyes and tousled orange hair. To his surprise, she held out her arms to him. Was he dreaming?

"Dave!" she breathed. "You're my hero!"

"He's not—oof!" Screech exclaimed, bending over as Zack's elbow caught him in the stomach. Zack reached over and took one of the girl's outstretched hands. He brushed his lips against it, and a ripple of admiration went through the three girls.

"Sorry, Sam," Zack said. "Girls, this is my manager, Samuel Powers."

"And you don't have to tell us who you are," a petite blonde said.

"We recognized you all the way across the room," the brunette said.

"No, girls," Screech said. "This is—ooooff!" Zack had elbowed him again.

"Sorry, Sam," Zack said. "I didn't notice you were standing right there." He tipped his hat and gave the three girls his most winning smile. "That's right, girls. I'm Daredevil Dave Laramie!"

▲ ▼ ▲

Everyone met at the car as planned, and Chance drove off into a blazing orange sunset. The gang chattered about how much they'd loved Santa Fe.

"I have to say, though, a horrible thing *did* happen," Lisa said. "I walked into a store, and someone was wearing the same exact outfit I had on. How do you like that—I travel a thousand miles and end up bumping into myself!"

Kelly laughed. "She didn't look anything like you, Lisa. She was about ten years older and fifty pounds heavier."

"That was the scary part," Lisa said. "Maybe she's a future me!"

Everyone laughed. "Coincidences are funny things," Jessie said. "Like when you look a lot like somebody else."

She waited for Chance to tell the story of how that woman was convinced he was someone named Chuck, but he kept his eyes on the road.

"They say that everybody in the world has a double," Jessie said. It was hard to see Chance in the dusky light, but he didn't seem to have any expression at all. He just kept driving.

Zack shot Jessie an apprehensive look. *What was she doing?* Had she been in the store when he was talking to those girls?

"That's just an old wives' tale," Zack said quickly.

"Gosh, Zack," Screech said, "are you volunteering at the senior center again? I thought they asked you not to come back after you organized that Jell-O volleyball game."

"I'm saying it's just a story, Screech," Zack said. "I wasn't really listening to old wives. It's just impossible for two people to have the same face."

"But today—oof," Screech said.

"I think it could be true," Jessie said.

"I wish it could," Lisa said. "Can you imagine if there were two Denzel Washingtons in the world?"

"Or two Brad Pitts?" Kelly said with a laugh.

"Or two Daredevil Dave Lar—ooof," Screech said.

Zack sighed. His elbow sure was getting a workout. He'd have to swear Screech to secrecy tonight. He probably shouldn't have pretended to be Daredevil Dave, but the girls were so thrilled to meet him. He hadn't wanted to disappoint them. And then, when they offered to take him to lunch tomorrow, he just couldn't say no. How could he let down his fans?

There was a funny tone in Jessie's voice as though she were a bloodhound chasing down a scent. Zack hadn't seen her in the store, and Jessie, with her wild curly hair and long legs, was hard to miss. Maybe the fact that she'd brought up two people having the same face was just a coincidence.

But just in case, he'd better be careful. Kelly wouldn't be too happy to find out he was impersonating a rodeo star and letting three girls take him to lunch. He'd have to think of a way to distract her.

Of course, the whole thing was completely harmless. After lunch, he'd never see those girls again. But he should be careful all the same.

▲   ▼   ▲

The Lazybones Ranch turned out to consist of a gorgeous adobe main house overlooking a courtyard with smaller cottages encircling it. These housed individual suites. Chance had given the boys one of the cottages, and he'd given the girls the one directly across the courtyard from it.

Each cottage had a large living room, with a kitchenette fully stacked with sodas and snacks, and an equally large bedroom. There was a Jacuzzi in the bathroom and thick, white terry-cloth robes for each guest. Both the bedroom and the living room had a fireplace with a basket of wood next to it.

"This is called piñon wood," Chance explained when he showed the girls their suite. "It's a kind of small pine tree, and the wood smells wonderful. If you run out, just dial the front desk and they'll deliver more. Sleep well," he said with a smile, and left the girls alone.

"Your mom is so lucky," Lisa sighed, flopping back on the couch.

"I know," Jessie said halfheartedly. Even though she knew what she'd seen had probably been nothing at all, she couldn't help feeling a little wary of Chance. It was just too weird.

Maybe tomorrow she would run into the woman in town. And maybe she could ask her just a few questions about this guy Chuck. Jessie sighed. If Slater were here, he'd tell her to mind her own business. But a few teeny questions to satisfy her curiosity couldn't hurt. She'd keep an eye out for the woman tomorrow. Most of the tourists stay in the hotels around the plaza. She'd probably bump into her sooner or later.

Kelly walked around to inspect the southwestern decorations. "Can you believe this place?" she asked, running her hand along a multicolored Indian blanket hung on the white wall. "It has everything. There's a pool, a steam room, a spa, and a gym. There are horses, hiking trails, and even a tennis court."

"How are we going to fit everything in?" Lisa asked.

"I don't know," Kelly said with a giggle. "But we'll have fun trying. I really want to go hiking and riding tomorrow."

"No, I mean the pedicure and the seaweed wrap and the hydrotherapy massage," Lisa said.

Kelly and Jessie groaned. "Lisa, you can't

spend your whole weekend indoors at the spa," Jessie said.

"Well, of course not," Lisa agreed. "I have to shop, too!"

Kelly and Jessie exchanged a hopeless glance. Lisa would never become the outdoorsy type, no matter where she went. While Jessie and Kelly were looking at mountains and trees, Lisa was wondering when they'd get to a mall.

Jessie yawned. "I'm really beat."

"Maybe we should turn in early," Kelly suggested. "Chance said there's a big breakfast buffet in the main house starting at seven-thirty, and it would be great to get an early start. There's so much I want to do tomorrow!"

"Exactly my point," Lisa agreed sleepily. "And I always say a pedicure starts the day off right."

Chapter 4

▼　▲　▼　▲　▼

Everyone gathered in the main house early the next morning. For breakfast, there were huevos rancheros, eggs with salsa and cheese, and blue-corn enchiladas. There were slices of thick, home-made bread for toast, jalapeño corn muffins, and warm corn tortillas. Finally, platters spilling over with sausage and black beans were brought out.

"I'm surprised this table doesn't collapse," Kelly laughed, looking at the long sideboard covered with hot food.

"This sure beats cereal for breakfast," Zack said, piling eggs and muffins on his plate.

"I'm glad you like it," Chance said. "I have the best cook in Santa Fe."

"Mmmmffffggg," Screech said.

Chance looked at the gang. "What did he say?"

Screech swallowed. "I said 'I'd agree with you, but I have my mouth full,'" he explained.

Slater forked up another bite of beans. "Chance, I went out for a walk to the stables this morning, and one of the ranch hands told me that you were sponsoring a rodeo here on Monday."

Zack looked up uneasily. *Rodeo?*

"That's right," Chance said. "I forgot to mention it yesterday. It should be fun."

Jessie swallowed. "A rodeo?"

"Yep," Chance said. "The whole town will show up, most likely. There'll be broncos, trick riding, and clowns . . . the whole shebang."

"But I thought you loved animals, Chance," Jessie said. "Rodeos are so cruel to them."

"Some are," Chance agreed. "That's why I was careful to check into this one when I agreed to sponsor it here. They have an excellent track record. No animals have ever been injured."

"But that doesn't mean it can't happen!" Jessie protested. "It's a terrible thing, to rope a cow and practically break its leg—"

"Jessie, that's enough," her mother said.

"But, Mom, we're in the Animal Rights League together," Jessie said. "You're not going to go to this thing, are you?"

"If Chance says he looked into it, I'm sure it's okay," her mother said.

Jessie's lips pressed together. Was this Kate Spano, animal rights activist, talking? What had happened to her mom? She was gazing goonily at Chance like he was the best thing since blue-corn enchiladas.

The rest of the gang started to talk about what to do that morning. They were used to Jessie's dedication to her ideals, even at breakfast.

After the meal, Jessie took Slater aside. "I have to talk to Mom," she said.

"But we're supposed to go riding together," Slater said. "I already reserved the horses." He peered at her knowingly. "Whoa. You're not going to talk to her about the rodeo, are you?"

Jessie nodded. "I can't help it, Slater. I don't understand why she's letting Chance walk all over her like that."

Slater opened his mouth and then closed it. "Fine," he said. "I'll head out to the stables with Kelly."

"I'll catch up with you guys," Jessie promised. She hurried up the stairs toward her mother's room overlooking the pool.

She knocked softly, and her mother called out to come in. She was slipping into a pair of hiking boots. "Hi, sweetie," she said when she saw Jessie. "Chance and I are going for a hike. Do you want to come?"

"No, thanks, Mom," Jessie said. "I'm supposed to go riding with Slater. But I wanted to talk to you first."

"Sure, hon," her mother said. She gave a quick glance in the mirror as she brushed her hair.

"What are you doing?" Jessie burst out.

"I'm brushing my hair," her mother said, surprised. "It's a little messy."

"No, I mean about the rodeo," Jessie said. "You were the one who got all upset and wrote an editorial in the Palisades *Gazette* after that rodeo came to town last year. What's happened to your principles?"

Her mother put down the brush. She sighed. "Jessie, come on. I haven't abandoned my principles. But we're guests of Chance's. I'm not about to picket the place. And I trust him. I know him. I've seen the respect he has for living things."

"Sure, as long as there isn't any way he could exploit them for a profit," Jessie grumbled.

"Jessie! That's not fair," her mother said. "And besides, the proceeds from the rodeo are going to a local charity. Chance isn't in this for the money."

"Oh," Jessie said, a little deflated. "But that

still doesn't make it right! And the mom I used to know would agree with me!"

Mrs. Spano sighed and sat down on the edge of the bed. "He's a good man, Jess. Give him a chance."

Jessie crossed her arms. "So I should just forget my principles."

Mrs. Spano gave Jessie a shrewd look. "Besides, I think you know that two people with different ideas about things can still fall in love. Don't you?"

Jessie flushed guiltily. It was true. Slater's idea of a political protest was to campaign for more cheese on the burgers in the cafeteria. They had practically nothing in common.

"In any relationship, there's room to disagree," Mrs. Spano said. "Am I right?"

"You're right, Mom," Jessie said finally.

"So we'll be polite about the rodeo and give Chance a break?"

"All right," Jessie said.

Her mother stood up and put her hand on Jessie's shoulder. "Please trust me on this, Jess. Chance is one of the good guys. Promise me you'll try to like him."

"I promise, Mom," Jessie said. "Have a good hike."

She slipped out of her mother's room and hurried to the stables. Her mother's words about Slater had reminded Jessie of how precious this weekend was. She wanted to spend every moment she could with Slater.

But Slater and Kelly had gotten tired of waiting. They'd already taken off down the trail with one of the ranch hands. The other hand told Jessie they had asked him to take her to them, but Jessie hesitated. She really couldn't ride very well. She'd just wanted to do it because Slater did. But now she could go to town and wander around before lunch, and maybe she'd see that woman again.

She went in search of Lisa, but Lisa had already gone to the spa for her complimentary pedicure and massage. Zack and Screech were nowhere to be found.

Jessie decided to head to town alone. She left a note in her room, reminding the girls that they had all planned to meet in town for lunch. Grabbing her purse, Jessie headed back to the stables to hitch a ride with one of the hands.

▲   ▼   ▲

"Thank you so much for meeting us, Dave," Tawnee gushed. She giggled behind a veil of hair and fixed her eyes on Zack. "I can't tell you what a thrill it is to be sitting here with you."

"Don't mention it, Tawnee," Zack said, gloating slightly. "I love to spend time with my fans." He smiled at the three pretty, adoring faces surrounding him. Screech had dropped him off and then gone exploring. He was trying to find a new pet for his lizard collection.

"Did you grow up on a ranch, Dave?" Crystal, the petite blonde, asked.

Zack nodded. "Brought up with horses all my life," he said. "Ranch life is tough, no question. But it makes a real man out of you."

"Dave, I'm really looking forward to seeing you ride in the rodeo on Monday," Tawnee said. "I can't believe how lucky we are to catch you the very weekend we're in Santa Fe."

"I guess you're one of the surprise guests they announced on the poster," Crystal said.

Zack gulped down a sip of iced tea. He toyed with his chicken tostada. "Uh, the rodeo? Actually, I'm not competing," he said.

"Why not?" Angel asked. "Isn't the St. Gabriel Children's Home your favorite charity?"

"I heard that," Tawnee said, nodding. "I was really touched when I read that you play Santa for the kids every Christmas."

"Oh, yes, the kiddies are very close to my heart, no question," Zack said quickly. "What I mean is, I *can't* be in the rodeo. I injured my . . . clavichord a couple of months ago."

Crystal frowned. "Your clavichord? What's that?"

Zack pointed to his left shoulder. "It's right here." He lifted his arm halfway. "If I lift my arm any more than this, I could permanently dislocate my harpsichord. It could snap," he said, snapping his fingers, "just like that."

The three girls exchanged glances. "Gosh," Tawnee said slowly. "That's awful."

Zack nodded solemnly. "That's the price you pay for being macho, Tawnee."

Tawnee leaned closer. "It must *kill* you to have to see other cowboys ride in the rodeo and get all the glory."

Zack nodded. "It's tough. But my doctor said no way, José, could I risk my health."

"Oh, I agree," Tawnee said. "I think you're really wise."

Zack took his last bite of the delicious chicken tostada piled with cheese and guacamole and garnished with green chili salsa. This was totally cool, to be surrounded by three babes who were worshiping their hero. He could definitely get used to this.

Just then Screech's curly head bobbed above

the other diners. He gestured at Zack. Zack nodded and smiled and then returned his attention to Tawnee.

"I'm so glad we got to meet you," Angel said.

Suddenly Screech appeared at the table. "Better *late* than never," he said, giving Zack a meaningful look. Zack had no idea what it meant.

"Ladies, you remember my manager, Sam Powers," Zack said. He frowned at Screech. "We were just finishing lunch, Sam. I'll meet you outside."

"Would you like some dessert, Dave?" Tawnee asked. "They have a terrific chocolate-chili cake here."

"Is it really *time* for dessert already?" Screech asked, leaning toward Zack and winking.

"I'm completely stuffed, but I can never resist chocolate cake," Zack said. "It's my fav—"

"That's a great sweater, Angel," Screech interrupted. "*Kelly* green is my favorite color."

Kelly! He was supposed to meet her and the rest of the gang on the plaza! He was late!

"As I was saying," Zack said, "chocolate cake sounds great, but I really have to be going. I've got the little children to visit, you know."

"Of course," Tawnee said. "I understand completely. Thanks for letting us take you to lunch, Dave. It was a thrill."

"I can't wait to tell everyone back in Boulder," Crystal said.

"It was the most exciting lunch of my life," Angel said. "And I'm including the time I was having a slice of pizza and saw Pete Pollinski picking up his laundry across the street."

"Gee, thanks, Angel," Zack said. "That really means a lot to me."

He said his good-byes. Kelly was the only girl for him, no question. But it sure was fun having a fan club!

He rushed out of the restaurant with Screech at his heels. As he hurried out onto the sidewalk, he saw Kelly crossing toward the plaza with Slater. Zack quickly bent down to tie his sneaker. Screech was coming up fast behind him and fell over him.

"Yeeow!" Screech yelped.

"Shhhh," Zack said out of the corner of his mouth. "Kelly's over there. I don't want her to see me coming out of a restaurant."

From his sprawled position on the sidewalk, Screech rubbed his elbow. "It's getting dangerous to be around you, Zack. I hope I make it back to Palisades in one piece."

Zack and Screech made their way to the plaza, where the others were already waiting.

"There you are!" Kelly called. "Where did you

disappear to this morning? I thought we were going riding."

"We must have gotten our signals crossed," Zack said. "Screech and I went to the museum."

"Which museum?" Kelly asked.

"Uh, the famous one," Zack said quickly. He rubbed his hands together. "So, what's on the agenda?"

"Lunch, definitely," Lisa said. "I had an exhausting morning."

"You got a massage," Slater pointed out.

"I know," Lisa said. "My muscles really got a workout."

"We're ready for lunch, too," Kelly said with a glance at Slater. "We had the most beautiful ride, but that mountain air really makes you hungry."

"What happened to you, Jessie?" Slater asked her. "We told the guy at the stables that you could catch up with us."

"I must have misunderstood your message," Jessie said quickly, "so I decided to come into town and walk around. I'm really hungry now, too. Let's eat. Chance told me we should try the Coyote Café."

Zack gulped. He'd just had lunch at the Coyote Café. "How about a hamburger, gang?" he urged. "Aren't you sick of southwestern food yet?"

"No way," Jessie said.

"I can't get enough," Lisa agreed.

"Why should we eat hamburgers when we have them in Palisades all the time?" Kelly said. "Let's go to the Coyote Café."

Zack trailed after the gang to the restaurant. The hostess showed them to the same table he'd sat at with Tawnee and the other two girls. When the waitress came by, she gave him a puzzled look.

"What will it be, folks?" she asked, her pencil poised over her pad.

"I'll have the vegetable burrito," Jessie said.

"Good choice," the waitress said.

"What else do you recommend?" Kelly asked.

"Well, the house special is our chicken tostada," the waitress replied. "The chicken is grilled over mesquite, and we top it with cheese, green chili salsa, and the best guacamole in Santa Fe. It comes with our famous stuffed chilies and spicy beans on the side."

"Sounds delicious," Kelly said. "I'll have that."

"Me, too," Lisa said.

"Sounds great to me," Slater said, closing his menu.

"Me, too," Screech agreed.

Zack waved a hand feebly. "I guess I'll make it easy."

The waitress tilted her head to check out Zack

more closely. She shook her head as she stuck her pencil behind her ear. "It's amazing you're able to keep in shape, eating the way you do," she said.

"Gee," Kelly said in a hushed tone as the waitress walked away. "I know people are really friendly in Santa Fe, but isn't that kind of a personal remark?"

"Oh, that was just because—ooooof!" Screech almost doubled over as Zack's elbow made its way into his stomach.

"Because she's probably a fitness freak," Zack finished. He rubbed his elbow. If Screech didn't keep his mouth shut, Zack really would damage his clavichord. Whatever that was.

Chapter 5

▼ ▲ ▼ ▲ ▼

Jessie finished the last bite of her burrito and looked out onto the busy street. Suddenly she sat up. The woman she'd been looking for was walking right past the window!

Jessie threw down her napkin and stood up. "I've got to go," she said to the gang.

A.C. looked up from his second helping of black beans. "You do? Where?"

"Um, I have to buy a pair of earrings," Jessie said.

"And I thought I was obsessed with shopping," Lisa said.

"I'll catch up with you guys later," Jessie said hurriedly.

"But we're supposed to—," Slater said, but Jessie was already dashing out.

She threaded through tables and slipped out the front door. The woman was already at the end of the block. But dressed in a hot-pink sequined sweatshirt, she was easy to spot.

Jessie hurried down the street. "Excuse me!" she called.

The woman turned. "Are you talking to me, honey?" She had a slight southern accent.

"Yes," Jessie said breathlessly. "I want to ask you something."

"Fire away," the woman said, smiling pleasantly. "I'm Madge Moxley, by the way."

"Jessie Spano," Jessie said. "I saw you talking to a man yesterday, and I thought I knew him. You were standing over by the newsstand on San Francisco Street."

"Of course, I remember," Madge said. "Big, handsome guy?"

"That's the one," Jessie said excitedly.

"I can't recall his name," the woman said, frowning. "Gamble? Risk? Something like that."

"Who did you *think* he was?" Jessie asked.

"Oh, that's easy. I thought he was an old friend of mine. Chuck MacGuffin. That guy Gambler was a dead ringer for him. A little older, maybe. Well, of course he would be, I knew Chuck MacGuffin back in eighty-six. But I didn't think another man could possess a pair of crystal blue eyes like Chuck's. I was wrong."

"Chuck MacGuffin," Jessie said. She furrowed her brow, pretending to frown. "That name sounds familiar."

"It might be, if you come from horse country in Virginia," Madge said. "It's too bad that that man wasn't Chuck, because I'd have liked to have told him that I never believed the stories about him one bit. Not even when he up and disappeared. No, sir."

"What did he do?" Jessie asked breathlessly.

Suddenly Madge seemed to realize she was talking to a perfect stranger. She waved a hand. "Oh, it's long past now, darlin'. You're too young to be worrying about some old story."

"No, really, I—"

"My, you're a pretty girl. Are you here with your boyfriend? I just saw a pair of silver earrings with green stones in that window over there. They'd bring out those emerald flecks in your eyes," Madge went on.

Though Madge spoke in a soft drawl, Jessie sensed the power of a bulldozer. The woman wasn't about to discuss the troubles of an old friend with a complete stranger.

"It was nice meeting you, Madge," she said with a sigh. "I'll look for those earrings."

Madge patted her shoulder. "You do that, honey. And go find your boyfriend. I'm going to toddle back to the Hilton for a nap. Enjoy your stay in Santa Fe."

Jessie watched Madge walk off. Her hazel eyes narrowed as she pondered what Madge had said. Madge had seemed to accept that Chance wasn't her friend, the mysterious Chuck MacGuffin. But what if he *was*? Her mother could be getting into something way over her head. Whatever the truth was, Jessie owed it to her mom to find it out.

▲   ▼   ▲

Zack strolled down the street with Kelly, hand in hand. It felt good to be with his girlfriend again. Now he remembered what he'd been looking forward to on this trip to Santa Fe: spending maximum quality time with his sweetie.

A few yards in front of them, a head of bright orange hair gleamed. A pair of long legs in faded jeans strolled. A familiar profile peeked around the curtain of shining hair—

Zack yanked Kelly's hand and pulled her over to the nearest shop.

"Zack!" Kelly protested. "What—"

"Look at that, Kelly. Isn't it beautiful?" Zack

said. His eyes were on the reflection in the window. Was Tawnee stopping? Was she going to turn around?

"Gosh, Zack, I didn't know you were interested in Native American pottery," Kelly said. "Because I—"

"Let's go inside," Zack said, and pulled Kelly through the doorway.

He guided Kelly toward the back of the gallery, away from the windows. "Look at these pots," he said distractedly. "I love these."

"Me, too," Kelly said. "They're so simple and beautiful."

Zack took her elbow and moved her farther toward the wall. "I just love these over here, too," he said.

"Really? On the way to the plaza, Slater and I were looking at some vessels by the window. Let me show you—"

"No! Look at these!"

Kelly giggled. "Gosh, Zack, you sound like the pottery dictator."

"Oh. Sorry, Kelly. It's just that I love these pots *so much*," Zack said, anxiously looking over Kelly's shoulder. To his horror, he saw Tawnee walk into the gallery. He turned quickly and pretended to study a row of pottery.

"I like that black one," Kelly said. "You know,

it's funny. I never really noticed this kind of thing before. But Slater was talking to me about the simplicity of lines and shapes. He really made me see how beautiful these are. I didn't realize that he knew about stuff like this. Isn't that interesting?"

"Mmmmm," Zack said, inching away toward the corner. Tawnee was strolling toward the back of the gallery.

"There's Slater now," Kelly said, twisting around. "Let's ask him to show us his favorites."

"No!" Zack said. "I mean, I just want to be alone with you, Kelly."

Kelly looked around the crowded gallery. "This isn't exactly the beach at sunset, Zack."

Tawnee moved toward the display opposite from Kelly and Zack. Any moment now, she would see him. Zack backed up.

"Zack!" Kelly called, horrified. "The shelf!"

Zack turned to see that he'd dislodged a shelf from its support. He reached out just in time as the shelf began to tilt. The pottery jumped and jangled. Kelly steadied it with shaking fingers.

"This pottery is *expensive*, Zack," she whispered.

Tawnee hadn't noticed the disturbance. Zack let out a relieved breath as she turned and walked out the door.

But someone else had seen. Slater was looking at him with one eyebrow raised. He turned and looked through the glass window at Tawnee as she walked by. Then he looked back at Zack again.

"Kelly, I've got to talk to Slater for a sec," Zack said. "I'll be right back."

Slater was already scowling as Zack walked up. "What's going on, preppy?" he asked. "I smell a scheme in the air."

"It's not a scheme," Zack told him. "I promise. It's just a . . . a case of mistaken identity that maybe went a little too far."

"*Maybe* went a little too far?" Slater asked sardonically.

"These girls think I'm a big rodeo star," Zack explained. "And I sort of went along with it. I just don't want Kelly to know."

"Why not?" Slater asked.

"You know why not," Zack said. "Kelly will get upset because I'm playing games again."

"I know how she feels," Slater said.

"Hang with me on this one, buddy," Zack said. "Tawnee and her friends think I'm this macho rodeo star. How can I walk away from this one? They *worship* me. Rodeo stars are big in the southwest, and they're from Colorado."

"I don't know about this, Zack," Slater said. "I'm sensing major trouble around the bend."

"No way. All I need for you to do is distract Kelly for me," Zack said. "I don't want to hurt Kelly's feelings. But I can't disappoint my fans, either. They worship Daredevil Dave. I can't let them down."

"You can't let *your fans* down," Slater repeated.

"Right. This is all for fun, and it's not really hurting anybody. So will you cover for me, pal? And will you keep an eye on Kelly when I'm not around?"

Slater just stared at him.

"Slater? A.C.? Buddy?" Why was Slater looking at him that way?

"Sure, Zack," Slater said tonelessly. "I'll cover for you. And I'll keep an eye on Kelly."

"You're a true pal," Zack said. "I knew I could count on you."

He rushed back to Kelly across the gallery. "Miss me?"

Kelly's blue eyes twinkled. "You bet, big guy. Did Slater tell you about the pottery?"

"Oh, yeah," Zack said. "You're right, he does know a lot. We had a very informative talk."

▲   ▼   ▲

Jessie told the gang what she'd found out from Madge Moxley as they were driving back to the ranch.

"I really think this is worth investigating, don't you?" she asked everyone. "I mean, I don't want Mom to get hurt."

"I don't know, Jessie," Slater said. "You're jumping into something that isn't really any of your business."

"Not my business? She's my *mother*," Jessie protested hotly.

"Exactly. She's your mother. She's older and smarter. I think Kate Spano can take care of herself," Slater responded calmly.

"Just because Mom is so together doesn't mean she can't get swindled by some crook," Jessie argued.

"Swindled by a crook?" Slater asked, incredulous. "Boy, are you jumping to conclusions. This lady Madge thinks he might look like someone she used to know. So what?"

"Someone who was accused of something terrible," Jessie said. "Someone who mysteriously disappeared."

Slater shook his curly head of hair. "Jessie, you're doing it again. You're rushing into something without thinking. Why don't you talk to Chance?"

Jessie snorted. "Why should I? If he is this guy Chuck, he won't admit it."

"How do you know that?" Kelly put in. "Your mom trusts him, Jessie. Why shouldn't you?"

Jessie stared stonily ahead. "Are you guys with me or not? Will you help me investigate Chance?"

Slater and Kelly sighed. "Of course we're with you," they said together.

"We'll help you," Zack promised.

"Certainly we will," Lisa said. "I can start right after my seaweed wrap."

Jessie smiled. "Thanks, guys. I knew I could count on you."

Zack pulled into the ranch parking lot, and everyone spilled out and headed for their rooms. The plan was to change and go for a swim in the heated pool.

Jessie hurried after Kelly. "Kelly!" she called.

Kelly turned, her long hair swinging. "What's up?"

"I wanted to ask you something," Jessie said in a low voice. "I'm probably going to be busy with this Chance thing. I know Slater isn't crazy about it. So would you kind of keep an eye on him for me? I don't want him to feel neglected."

Kelly frowned. "Jessie, don't you think that *you* should make sure Slater doesn't feel neglected? He's *your* boyfriend."

"Are you going to help me or not?" Jessie asked.

"Of course I'll help you," Kelly assured her. "It's just that—"

"Thanks," Jessie said. "You're a true pal. I knew I could count on you."

Chapter 6

▼ ▲ ▼ ▲ ▼

Later that afternoon, Jessie and Lisa drove back into town while the others went with Chance and Mrs. Spano to an old mission several miles away. Jessie and Lisa had managed to beg off, saying that they were going to nap.

Jessie drove straight to the library in town. "I can't believe I'm doing this," Lisa sighed. "I'm actually going to the library on my vacation."

"Thanks for helping me, Lisa," Jessie said.

"Don't mention it," Lisa said. "Anything for you, girl. But next time you want to do some investigating, try to do it in a mall, okay?"

Jessie led the way into the library. While Lisa checked the stacks for cute guys, Jessie talked to the librarian. While Lisa went to get a soda, Jessie hooked into the library's computer network. And while Lisa was in the ladies' room freshening her makeup, Jessie found what she was looking for.

"Look," she told Lisa excitedly when she returned. "I found an article in a Virginia newspaper from nineteen eighty-six. I cross-referenced the name MacGuffin and looked for horse breeding stories because Madge said he came from horse country. It turns out that a guy named Chuck MacGuffin owned a thoroughbred breeding farm in Virginia."

"So, that's good, right?" Lisa said. "We can go back to the ranch. This really cute ranch hand is going to teach me how to throw a lariat."

"Lisa, you're not listening to me," Jessie said. "The police investigated this guy MacGuffin. He was accused of drugging a horse before a race."

"Well, that doesn't really mean anything," Lisa said slowly. "They couldn't prove it, right?"

Jessie scanned the article again. "They know the horse was drugged. He died of a heart attack in the middle of the race. But charges were never filed."

"You see?" Lisa said, relieved. "Now can we head back? It's going to get dark soon."

Jessie frowned as she switched off the computer. "What I really need is a picture of MacGuffin. Then I'd have proof."

"Proof of what?" Lisa said, swinging her purse onto her shoulder. "You said they couldn't prove anything. Even if you prove that Chance is Chuck, that doesn't mean he's a criminal."

"There just has to be more to the story," Jessie said.

"Sure," Lisa said. "But how can we find out anything? There's no evidence pointing a finger at Chuck, not to mention Chance."

"Tell me this then, Lisa," Jessie said. She leaned closer and lowered her voice. "If Chuck MacGuffin wasn't guilty, why did he leave his home and his business?" Jessie tapped the computer, her hazel eyes intense. *"Why did Chuck MacGuffin disappear?"*

▲   ▼   ▲

Kelly surfaced in the middle of the indoor pool and smiled across the warm water at Slater.

"You were right. A swim before dinner is perfect."

"Especially after that dusty trail around the mission," Slater said.

"It was dusty, but it was worth it," Kelly said as she lazily did the breaststroke toward him. "Those wildflowers were incredible."

She swam up to where Slater was lounging by the side of the pool. The sun was setting outside the glass walls of the pool house, and drops of water glinted in Slater's dark curls. The pool room felt steamy and snug.

Kelly leaned against the side of the pool and cupped her face in her hands. "I hope Jessie's wrong about Chance," she said. "I really like him."

"I like him, too," Slater said. "He's a cool guy. Maybe she doesn't want to like him."

"What do you mean, Slater?" Kelly asked.

He shrugged. "I'm not sure. But Jessie seemed a tad too eager to nail this guy. Maybe she doesn't really want her mom to have a man in her life. She's ragged on every single one of her mom's boyfriends. They're not smart enough, or hip enough, or they wear dorky shoes."

Kelly laughed. "I know. But that guy Roger did wear dorky shoes, Slater."

Slater laughed, too. "Yeah, he did."

Kelly trailed a finger in the water. "I haven't seen much of Zack this weekend so far. So much for a romantic weekend."

"Tell me about it," Slater groaned. "I'm beginning to think that Jessie is a figment of my imagination."

Kelly watched her hand move across the still water. "But I have to admit, I'm having a good time, anyway," she said. "Talking to you about the Native American pottery was neat. And I didn't realize you knew the names of so many plants. Jessie never told me you knew about that kind of stuff."

Slater shrugged. "I've got a few hobbies Jessie doesn't know about."

Kelly saw that she'd embarrassed Slater a little bit. He didn't seem to like being the kind of guy who knew about ceramic art or the names of flowers. But this weekend, she'd seen a more sensitive side to him that she really liked.

Slater looked down at Kelly's dark hair. It was wet, and it looked as dark and shiny as ebony. He couldn't believe that Zack didn't want to spend every minute he could with this fantastic girl.

Not that Slater didn't love Jessie. But he'd been having so much fun with Kelly this weekend. She was happy doing anything: riding horses, hiking, shopping, or just hanging out. She didn't have an agenda, like Jessie. She didn't plan out her leisure time as though it was study period at school. Fifteen minutes for the French quiz, a half hour for chemistry, twenty minutes to go over history notes. Jessie approached her whole life like that.

Kelly was easy to be with. She was smart and funny, but she didn't hit you over the head with her intelligence.

And his best friend, Zack, was a big jerk.

"Well, I guess we'd better get back to our rooms," Kelly said. She started to push herself out of the pool.

"Let me help you," Slater said. He bent down and grabbed hold of her waist and then pulled her out of the pool. As she came out of the water, she slid against his bare chest and stepped on his foot. They both backed up quickly, laughing a little.

"Oops," Kelly said. "Sorry."

"It's fine," Slater said. He could still feel the slick, satiny texture of her wet skin.

"Slater?" Kelly looked at him, puzzled. "Are you okay?" Kelly wasn't sure how she felt herself. A little dizzy maybe, from being pulled up so quickly. Or had it been the feel of his strong hands around her waist?

"I'm fine," Slater said. "Just fine."

Kelly shivered and reached for her towel. "Maybe I'll stop by and see if Zack's headache is any better."

"Maybe you shouldn't," Slater said. "I mean," he added hurriedly when Kelly gave him a puzzled look, "it's almost time for dinner. And the sun is going down. You might catch cold."

A mischievous grin spread over Kelly's face. "Or maybe I wouldn't find him in his room?" she asked Slater.

"W-what do you mean?" Slater said. "He said he was going to take an aspirin and lie down."

"Mmmm," Kelly said. "Or maybe while you and I went for a swim, he decided to go to town."

"Why would he do that?" Slater said warily.

Kelly gave a resigned sigh. "Slater, I know Zack is up to something."

He gulped. "You do?"

Kelly slipped her long T-shirt over her tank suit. "Boy, am I sick of everyone thinking I'm stupid," she said.

"Kelly, I don't think you're stupid," Slater burst out. "I think you're smart and funny and . . . and wonderful." He blushed. "I mean, why do you say I think you're stupid?"

"Because I've been going out with Zack on and off for years, and I've known him all my life," Kelly said. "Do you really think that I'm so stupid that I can't tell when he's hiding something from me? Of course I can. I don't know exactly what he's up to, but I bet it has something to do with that redhead who was in the gallery earlier today. Zack nearly broke a thousand dollars' worth of pottery trying to hide her from me."

"Zack isn't going out with her or anything," Slater said. "It's just that she thinks he's this big rodeo star—"

Kelly waved a hand. "Don't bother with the details. They're never important. What *is* important is that Zack is lying to me again. Sure, he'll say it's harmless. He'll say it's just so I won't get hurt or something."

"He doesn't mean any harm," Slater said.

Kelly shrugged. "He never means any harm, Slater. But something always blows up in his face. Once upon a time, I used to try to warn him. But I can't do it anymore. I'm tired of running after him, trying to talk him out of things. Zack is a big boy. He'll learn the hard way."

"You know what, Kelly?" Slater said. "I know exactly how you feel. I'm tired of trying to talk sense into Jessie, too. I'm tired of trying to get her to see both sides of things. I feel like I spend most of my time arguing with her. Look at her now. She's going after Chance like she's a federal prosecutor. I have a feeling she's heading for trouble, but what can I say? A big fat nothing."

"Exactly," Kelly said.

The two of them sighed gloomily. Then Kelly turned to Slater.

"So let's do something really revolutionary," she said. "This weekend, let's have fun. You and me. And let Zack and Jessie do whatever they have to. Let's not chase after them or try to talk them out of anything. Here we are in this beautiful place. Let's not let them spoil it."

"It's a deal, partner," Slater said. He held out his hand, and Kelly shook it.

He picked up her towel and looped it around her shoulders. Kelly stood there, smiling at him. He grinned back. And then, suddenly, a terrible thought popped into Slater's head.

He wanted to kiss her.

But she was his best friend's girl!

Kelly's blue eyes widened. Her lips parted as a surprised breath escaped her.

Slater was looking at her as if he wanted to kiss her. And she wanted him to!

But he was her best friend's guy!

Kelly took a step backward.

Slater cleared his throat.

"We'd better go," Kelly said. She felt like she'd said it about five times already. But she didn't *want* to go.

"Right," Slater said. He picked up his towel. The last thing he wanted to do was go. Who knew when he'd be alone with Kelly again? But maybe he shouldn't be alone with her. Because a guy could only be so good for so long. If he was alone with her again, he just might go ahead and kiss her.

They walked out into the crimson of a New

Mexican sunset. Normally Kelly would have commented on how beautiful it was. Slater would probably have pointed out how the mountains were turning deep purple.

But neither one of them said anything. Because they'd walked into the pool area as good friends and walked out as something different. Suddenly nothing was the same.

Then they heard their names called. Kelly and Slater jumped guiltily as Jessie and Zack waved at them from across the yard.

They stopped as Zack and Jessie hurried toward them.

"Hi!" Jessie called. "Did you have a good swim?"

"Fine," Slater said. He felt like he'd said the word a thousand times today.

"How's your headache?" Kelly asked Zack.

"All gone," he said. He shifted uncomfortably. Instead of resting in his room, he'd driven to the girls' hotel and played pool with them. Even though he wasn't really interested in any of them romantically, he couldn't help enjoying their adulation. It was definitely cool being someone else for a while who also happened to be famous. Zack couldn't help wanting to continue the charade, could he?

But at least Slater was looking out for Kelly. What a friend!

"I'm looking forward to the cookout tonight," Kelly said. "Chance is really going all out for us. And he said we'll never see as many stars as we will tonight."

Jessie pressed her lips together so that she wouldn't say anything mean about Chance. Something about the way Slater looked warned her off. He was walking beside her, but he might as well have been a million miles away. It was probably because she had spent this afternoon in the library.

But Kelly had come through. She'd made sure Slater was busy and having fun. What a friend!

Kelly felt Slater walking on the other side of Jessie. She sneaked a look at him. What was he thinking? Did he know that she wanted to kiss him? If she was back in Palisades, she'd fill her days with cheerleading or studying to distract herself from this very inconvenient attraction.

But she was miles away from home, and she'd just made a deal to spend lots of time with the guy she probably should avoid. Because in just one moment, with just one look, Slater had turned into one major temptation.

Was her bargain with Slater the best idea she'd ever had, or was she courting complete disaster?

Chapter 7

▼　▲　▼　▲　▼

The tantalizing aroma of sizzling steaks hit the gang's nostrils as soon as they left their rooms. Across the lawn, they could see torches flickering. Their path to the barbecue area was lit by what Chance called luminaria, candles in paper bags. They cast a romantic glow in the dusky light.

Chance had invited all of the guests at the ranch to the cookout. Groups of people were gathered by the outdoor pool, where drinks and snacks had been set up.

As the gang approached the barbecue area, they saw Chance with Rosa, the chef, and her helpers. Chance was chopping jalapeño peppers for Rosa's salsa.

"Rosa is letting me help tonight," he called to

the gang. His face was lit with a boyish grin. "She won't let me in her kitchen, but when we cook out, I get to help."

Mrs. Spano appeared out of the shadows, carrying a tall glass of iced tea. "There's sodas and chips and things by the pool," she told the gang. "Be sure and taste Rosa's guacamole. It's the best I've ever had."

Jessie approached her mother. "Can we talk for a minute?" she asked in a low voice.

"Sure, sweetie. Let's watch Chance cut that onion. I love to watch a grown man cry," her mother said, grinning.

"Can we go over there? On that bench?" Jessie asked, pointing to a bench underneath a large tree.

"Okay," Mrs. Spano said. She followed Jessie to the wrought-iron bench and sat down. Taking a deep breath of pine-scented air, she turned to her daughter. "Isn't this the most beautiful place on earth, Jess?"

"I guess," Jessie said. "I like Palisades, too."

"Oh, I love Palisades," her mother replied. "I love the ocean. But I could get used to the mountains as well."

"Mom, I need to tell you something," Jessie blurted. "I think I found out something about Chance."

Her mother seemed to freeze. She put her

glass down on the flagstones by the bench. "And what's that, Jessie?"

"Well, that he may not be what he seems to be," Jessie said. "I mean, he seems to be trustworthy and nice and all—"

"He *is* all of those things," her mother said evenly.

"But what if he isn't?" Jessie asked fervently. "What if he's fooling all of us? What if he's just pretending to be good so that you'll fall in love with him?"

"Not this again, Jessie," her mother said in an annoyed tone. "I know you hate that Chance is going to sponsor the rodeo. Maybe if you would just stop for a minute and give him a chance, he'd surprise you. If you didn't fly off the handle and just talked to him, you'd see what a good person he is. Maybe you'd even change his mind—or yours. Who knows?"

"Mom, it's not the rodeo," Jessie said. "It's him."

"Jessica Amelia Spano, that's enough," her mother said in the crisp, no-nonsense voice Jessie didn't hear very often. "I'm going to say something to you, and I want you to listen up: Mind your own business."

"This is my business!" Jessie said. "You might marry this guy!"

"That's right," Mrs. Spano said. "So let me make my own decision."

"But if you don't have all the facts—"

"Jessie, we went through this when your father met Leslie. You kept on talking about what a bad woman she was. How she was materialistic and shallow and a complete airhead—"

Jessie shifted uneasily. She had said all of those things. She wished now that she had kept her big mouth shut.

"—and now you think she's the best thing since tofu burgers. But because you couldn't stand the thought of your dad marrying her, you made them both miserable for months. Remember?"

"I remember," Jessie said. "I was wrong. I was a baby. I admit it. But this is diff—"

"No, it's not," her mother said firmly.

"It *is*," Jessie insisted. "Mom, it's just like the rodeo thing. He says he loves animals and horses, and then he sponsors a rodeo. *He isn't what he seems.*"

Her mother stood up. "That's enough, young lady. I don't want to hear one more word." She looked down at her daughter, and her features softened. "Honey, I know you're looking out for me. But aren't you telling me all the time that *I* have to let *you* make your own choices and maybe your own mistakes?"

Jessie nodded.

"Well, don't you think you should do the same for me?"

"But—," Jessie said weakly. Now she knew that she couldn't tell her mother about the clippings from the Virginia newspaper. Not yet. Not until she had absolute proof that Chance was Chuck MacGuffin. Her mom would just say that it was a coincidence. Or that Jessie was poking her nose in where she didn't belong. She wouldn't believe it. Not yet.

"No buts," her mom said. "Come on. Let's go back to the party. Let's forget we had this conversation. Chance made sure to have plenty of swordfish for you. He knows you don't eat meat. We're going to have a delicious dinner, and we're all going to get along. Right?"

Jessie nodded and stood up. But as she followed her mother back to the warm, glowing light of the lanterns, she suddenly had an idea. She knew how she would get proof that Chance Gifford was Chuck MacGuffin. Then everyone would realize that she wasn't on a wild-goose chase. They'd see she'd been right about sneaky Chance Gifford all along!

▲ ▼ ▲

"That was the best swordfish I've ever had," Kelly said.

"The steak was fantastic," Slater agreed. His eyes met Kelly's, and they both quickly looked away.

"So what's up for tomorrow?" Kelly asked brightly. "I know I want to hit the trails again. How about you, Zack?"

Zack was lying back on a chaise lounge by the pool, looking up at the stars. He remembered how the girls had hung on every word "Dave" had said. They'd bought him sodas and even let him win at pool.

"Zack?"

When they'd said good-bye to him, they'd practically begged him to come back. "Will we see you tomorrow, Dave?" Tawnee'd asked. "Please come by for a swim."

"Zack?"

Screech poked him. "Dave," he hissed.

Zack bolted upright. "What?"

"Do you want to go riding tomorrow?" Kelly repeated.

Zack thought fast. "You know what, Kelly? I discovered a weird thing. I think I'm allergic to horses. Every time I get around the corral, I start to sneeze."

"That is weird," Kelly said. "You and I have gone horseback riding in Palisades."

"Maybe it's just New Mexican horses," Zack said. "Anyway, I don't think I should ride tomorrow. Why don't you and Slater go?"

"I'm kind of tired of riding," Slater said.

"I'm not sure I really want to go," Kelly said at the same time.

"Why don't you guys come lizard hunting with me?" Screech suggested.

Lisa shuddered. "That's barbaric, Screech. I'm going to get the sea-salt scrub and then lie in a mud bath."

Kelly laughed. "*That* sounds pretty barbaric to me," she said.

"So what do you guys want to do tomorrow?" Lisa asked.

"Let's go to town," Kelly and Slater said at the same time. They looked at each other.

"Or maybe I'll stay at the ranch," Kelly said.

"What does Jessie want to do?" Zack said. "Where is she, anyway?"

"She's been jumping up and down all night," Slater said sourly. "I think she's keeping an eye on Chance and her mother. Like he's suddenly going to spirit her mother away into the desert or something."

"I bet Jessie will want to go riding," Zack said. "Okay, it's decided. Slater, Jessie, and Kelly go riding. Screech and I go to town. And Lisa gets to play with mud."

"Mud and sea salt," Lisa corrected. "But, actually, I think I'll go to town with you guys. I'd rather shop."

"Are you sure?" Zack asked.

Lisa gave him a deadpan look. "Honey, I'd *always* rather shop."

"Great," Zack said. He flopped back on his chair and regarded the starry sky. With Lisa tagging along, how was he going to manage to see his fans? Lisa would run back and tell Kelly what was going on in a New York minute. Zack sighed. It was awful how sometimes you just couldn't trust your friends at all.

▲   ▼   ▲

The next day after a big breakfast, Slater went to the girls' suite to pick up Jessie and Kelly on the way to the stables. But when he got there, Jessie was still in her robe.

"What's up?" he said. "I reserved the horses for ten o'clock."

Jessie pulled him inside. "Slater, do you have any idea how hard it is to find a place to fax something on a Sunday? All the copy shops are closed. I've been calling around since early this morning."

"I can solve the problem for you in two seconds," Slater said. "The ranch has its own fax machine. Just leave the fax at the front desk."

"But I need an answer!" Jessie said.

"They'll deliver it right to your room," Slater said. "So giddap, momma. Let's hit the trail."

"But I can't use the ranch's fax," Jessie said worriedly. "What if Chance sees it? Or what if he sees the reply?"

Slater sighed. "Then this is about Chance."

"Of course it is," Jessie said. "The thing is, I did find one copy shop right outside of town that opens at noon. So I can go there."

She pulled Slater down next to her on the couch. "Listen. I had this brainstorm last night. I called the Virginia paper this morning and asked them to find the original notes for the story they wrote. They say if I fax them all the information, they'll fax me back a photo if they have it! I said I was a reporter researching a story."

"So you want to wait around for a fax all day?" Slater asked.

Jessie nodded. "Slater, don't you see? If the photo of Chuck MacGuffin looks like Chance, I can take it to Mom. It will be proof that Chance is a criminal hiding out!"

Slater sighed. "Jessie, we've been here two days and two nights and we haven't spent any time together at all."

"I know," Jessie said. "And I'm sorry about that. I really wanted to have a romantic weekend with you. But, Slater, I can't ignore this! This is my mom's future we're talking about."

"I know you can't ignore it," Slater said. "But can't you sandwich in some *fun* once in a while?"

Jessie shook her head irritably. "No, I can't. I've got to get to the bottom of this. Why can't you understand that?"

Staring at Jessie, Slater counted to ten. He felt like he'd had this argument with her too many times. Kelly was right; it was tiring having to argue a person out of doing something all the time.

"Okay, Jess," he said softly. "Whatever you want."

A relieved smile broke over Jessie's face. "Great. I'll see you later, okay?"

"Sure," Slater said.

Just then Kelly came out of the bedroom dressed in faded jeans and her old cowboy boots. "All set," she said. She looked at Jessie's robe. "Oops. I guess one of us isn't. We'll wait for you, Jess."

"I'm not going," Jessie said. "I already explained to Slater." She stood up and knotted her robe determinedly. "So I have just enough time to shower and get to the library to photocopy my materials so I can fax all the stuff to the paper in Virginia."

"Wait, Jessie," Kelly said nervously. "Are you sure you can't go riding first?"

"No way," Jessie said. "I have oodles of stuff to do. You guys have fun! I'll see you later." She rushed into the bedroom.

Slater looked at Kelly. "I guess it's just the two of us," he said.

Kelly nodded. Her voice came out faintly. "I guess it is."

Chapter 8

▼　▲　▼　▲　▼

"Look at that adorable dress," Lisa said. "Do you like the blue or the yellow?"

"Blue," Screech said. "No, yellow. I really like you in yellow."

Zack rolled his eyes. It was harder than he thought it would be to slip away from Lisa in town. And the only reason was because Screech had suddenly turned into her best girlfriend. He had cheerfully followed her from store to store. No matter what excuses Zack came up with to disappear, Screech would squelch them. He was totally intent on pleasing Lisa.

Zack should have known better. Screech adored Lisa. If pretending to be interested in the benefits of a linen-cotton-ramie blend meant he could spend the day with her, he'd become Monsieur Screech, her very own personal fashion consultant.

Screech held up a blouse. "Look at this, Lisa! I think you should definitely try it on."

"Oooo, it's gorgeous," Lisa said. "I love green."

Screech eyed it critically. "I'd say it was more of a sage, myself."

"Exactly," Lisa beamed. "Wait right here, okay? I want you to tell me if it looks good on me."

"Then we can pick out some silver earrings to go with it," Screech said.

"Fabuloso!" Lisa squealed. She grabbed the blouse and ducked into the dressing room.

"Screech, what do you think you're doing?" Zack hissed.

"I'm coordinating," Screech said, holding up a multicolored gauze scarf. "Do you think this would go with that blouse?"

Zack grabbed the scarf and tossed it back on the counter.

"You're right," Screech said. "It really was too puce."

"Screech!" Zack said, backing him into a corner. "You are driving me crazy! I'm trying to give Lisa the slip!"

"Gosh, Zack, I'd be too embarrassed to shop

for lingerie for her," Screech said. "I mean, slips are kind of personal, don't you think?"

Zack clutched his head and groaned. He fixed Screech with a steely glare. "I'm trying to distract Lisa so that I can go find Tawnee and her friends."

"Oh," Screech said. "So what's stopping you?"

"*You* are!" Zack exclaimed. "Lisa said she wanted to see that movie, and you told her it was silly to see a movie on vacation when there was so much else to do. Then she wanted to go wander alone in the museum, and you told her she'd probably get bored by herself. Then she wanted to go to the old church on the plaza so that she could get in touch with her spirituality, and you said that there were only four shopping hours left because the stores close early today. You're driving me crazy!"

"I'm sorry, Zack," Screech said. "I guess I lose my head where Lisa's concerned."

"That's for sure," Zack said. "Now help me think of a good excuse to get out of here, will you? I have a vested interest in seeing Tawnee again."

"A vest! That's what Lisa needs!" Screech exclaimed. "I saw a darling black velvet one over there. . . ."

Screech rushed off, and Zack groaned again. He'd never get away without Lisa becoming suspicious! Screech was no help at all.

Lisa bought the blouse, the vest, and a pair of silver earrings Screech had picked out. She vetoed a fringed scarf and hesitated over a sweater. By the time she was finished, it was time to meet everyone back at the ranch.

"Gosh, Screech," Lisa said excitedly as they loaded her packages into the car, "I never knew you were so excellent at shopping. Maybe you'd like to take a couple of mall trips with me?"

"Anytime," Screech vowed.

On the drive back to the ranch, Zack wondered if he was going to be Daredevil Dave again. Tomorrow was the rodeo, and they were leaving that afternoon. Tonight Chance had planned a big farewell dinner at the ranch and a moonlight walk to look at the stars. Zack figured he was back to being plain old Zack Morris.

As they drove through the ranch entrance, they saw that the driveway and stable area were full of huge trailers. Muscular ranch hands were unloading bulls and horses down the ramps.

"It must be the rodeo," Lisa said. "Look! Those broncos look fierce."

Five burly hands were carefully leading a spirited black stallion down the ramp. Suddenly he bucked, and one of the men flew off the ramp and landed in the dust. Lisa squealed and covered her eyes.

"Don't worry, Lisa," Screech said masterfully. "He's okay."

"Can you imagine getting on that horse and riding it?" Lisa breathed. "Those guys must be crazy!"

Zack nodded speechlessly. Maybe it *was* lucky he wasn't Daredevil Dave. If he had to ride one of those bucking broncos, he'd end up punching his own personal hole in the ozone layer!

▲　▼　▲

Jessie stood impatiently in the copy shop. She'd hung around waiting for the fax until the woman at the desk had told her to go next door to the diner because Jessie was making her nervous. The clerk promised she'd call and tell her when the fax came in. Jessie had drunk three cups of hot chocolate until she got too anxious to stay any longer. What if the clerk forgot to call her? Jessie hurried back to the copy shop, but the fax hadn't come in yet.

The clerk at the counter looked pointedly at Jessie's tapping foot. Jessie stood still.

"Are you sure you don't want another hot chocolate?" the woman asked her.

"I can't," Jessie said.

"It's on me," the woman said.

"I really can't drink anymore," Jessie said. "I feel like I'm going to float away."

"We could only hope," the woman muttered, but she was interrupted by a beeping noise.

"My fax!" Jessie cried. "Thank goodness!"

"You said it," the woman murmured as she pulled out the fax and looked at the name on the top. "Yup, it's for you."

Jessie gave the woman her money and eagerly reached for the fax. She bit her lip as she squinted at the grainy photograph. "I *think* it's him," she murmured to herself. The man definitely looked like a slimmer, younger version of Chance. But he was half turned from the camera, and it was really hard to tell.

She looked up at the woman. "Thanks a lot," she said. "I'm sorry I made you nervous."

"Don't mention it," the woman said. "I hope you got the answer you were looking for."

"Oh, I did," Jessie said. She looked at the photograph again. "Sort of."

She tucked the photo in her backpack and walked out to get her bike. As she pedaled back to the ranch, Jessie decided that the photograph was of Chance. It was too much like him not to be him. And the coincidences were piling up just too fast.

She pulled into the driveway and stopped her bike as she saw the animals being led into Chance's stables. She felt so sorry for them!

Behind her, a group of locals had come out to watch the rodeo trucks being unloaded.

"Looks like it's going to be a good show this year," one of them said.

"Did you join the pool, Ed?" his friend said. "I put fifty down on Jimmy Ray Jones."

"Too rich for my blood," someone else said. "I just bet a deuce."

"I put down two fifty on Dusty Quint," another voice said. "Nothing can throw him. You ought to join me, Bob. The whole town is betting on Dusty."

Jessie wrinkled her nose in distaste. She was definitely opposed to people betting on animals. It just wasn't right, in her opinion. She wondered if Chance had bet on the rodeo, too. She snorted. What was she thinking? He was probably leading the betting pool! In his other life as Chuck MacGuffin, he'd been involved with horse racing, hadn't he? And look what name he'd picked for his new disguise—Chance! Oh, he was a gambler, all right.

Suddenly Jessie froze as the thought entered her brain. Everything seemed to add up with lightning speed.

Chuck MacGuffin had drugged a horse in order to win a bet. *What if Chance Gifford was planning to do the very same thing tomorrow?*

▲   ▼   ▲

The gang gathered in the living room of the girls' suite before dinner. A fire blazed in the fireplace, and the piñon wood crackled.

Jessie spread the photo out on the coffee table. "You see? It's Chance."

Slater frowned. "I don't know. It could be him."

"Then again, it might not," Lisa said.

"What do you think, Kelly?" Jessie asked.

Kelly peered at the photo. "I just don't know," she confessed. "It looks kind of like Chance."

"He's too skinny," Zack said.

Screech bristled. "What's wrong with skinny?"

"I mean he's skinnier than Chance," Zack said.

"But this was taken eight years ago," Jessie said. "He's younger in this picture."

Lisa sighed. "He was just as handsome back then."

"I should show this to my mom, right?" Jessie demanded, looking at them.

Slater shook his head. "I don't think so. It's not like it's hard evidence."

"It really could be anybody," Kelly said.

"And if Madge confused Chance with Chuck, that's why," Zack said. "The two men look alike."

Jessie angrily folded up the paper. "Don't you

think it's a coincidence that Chance offered to host the rodeo? What if he bet on one of the rodeo stars to lose? And what if he makes sure of it by drugging the horse or the bull? He has a perfect opportunity. All the animals are right in his stable!"

"Jessie, all you have are a lot of coincidences," Slater said. "That doesn't make them facts."

Jessie dug into the pocket of her jeans. "How about this then?" she asked. She brought out a bottle and slapped it on the table.

"What's that?" Lisa asked. "Vitamins?"

"Horse tranquilizers," Jessie announced. "I found them in Chance's stable." She looked at the faces of the gang. "Now tell me he's not up to something."

Slater hesitated. "Those could be for a sick horse."

"But *none of the horses are sick*," Jessie said. "And look, the bottle is dated for last week, right before we came."

The gang sat, staring at the bottle. Zack unfurled the fax and smoothed out the creases. He looked at the picture again.

"The point is," Jessie said, "what if Chance *is* planning to drug one of the animals? Shouldn't we do something about it?"

"Like what?" Kelly asked.

"Like stake out the stables tonight after our

hike," Jessie said. "Wait until everyone's gone to bed and then take turns out there."

Lisa shivered. "It gets awfully cold at night."

"So we'll take blankets," Jessie said. "What do you say, gang? Are you with me or not?"

Everybody hesitated. They looked at Jessie's determined face. Jessie might be jumping to conclusions, but she was still their friend.

"We're with you," they said.

▲　　▼　　▲

As soon as Zack got back to the boys' suite, he dialed Tawnee's hotel. She answered the phone on the first ring.

"Dave!" she cried when she heard his voice. "It's great to hear from you."

"I was hoping to come by for a swim like I promised," Zack said. "I got hung up at the St. Gabriel Children's Home. They wanted me to teach them how to throw a lariat."

"But what about your clavichord?" Tawnee asked, concerned.

"I, uh, was real careful," Zack said.

"Well, I understand completely," Tawnee said. "I know you're a big star and everything. You have to be kind to your fans."

"Thanks for being so understanding," Zack said.

"Well, how about dinner tonight?" Tawnee asked. "We're going to eat here at the hotel."

"I already have dinner plans," Zack said, disappointed. "It's a testimonial thing to honor me. You know how it is."

"Of course," Tawnee said sympathetically. "But, oooh, I'm so disappointed."

"Me, too," Zack said.

"Hey, wait—I have an idea! After dinner tonight, there's a country and western jamboree in the lounge. We're all going. Why don't you come, too, Dave? It'll be fun."

"It sounds like fun." Zack didn't exactly know what a jamboree was, but he wasn't about to ask. He was sure Daredevil Dave Laramie would know. "I'll tell you what, Tawnee. I'll really try to make it. But you know how long testimonial dinners can be."

"Not really," Tawnee said. "But I can imagine. We'll all look out for you, Dave. Especially me," she added softly.

Zack swallowed as he hung up the phone. Tawnee was really convinced he was Daredevil Dave. He had to find a way to see her tonight. He just had to.

Chapter 9

▼　▲　▼　▲　▼

It was late when the gang got back from their walk under the stars. They trudged back to their suites, wishing they could climb into their warm, soft beds with a piñon fire crackling across the cozy room. All except for Jessie. She was full of energy.

"I can't believe how long Chance kept us out on that trail," she grumbled. "He must have known every single constellation in the sky."

"I think it was interesting," Kelly said. "Especially all the Native American myths he knew."

"He was probably just trying to tire us out," Jessie said. "Maybe he suspects that we're on to him."

"Or maybe he's just an astronomy nut," Slater said.

"Anyway, we'll have to split up," Jessie said. "There's a lot of area to cover. Those stables are huge. We'll have to pair off."

Kelly looked at Zack expectantly, but he avoided her gaze.

"I have an idea," Zack said, thinking fast. "But I don't think anybody's going to like it. I don't even like it."

"What is it, Zack?" Kelly asked. She had a feeling she knew what was coming. Zack was going to figure out a way he could disappear without her knowing.

"If we really want to catch this guy, I don't think we should pair up in pairs," Zack said. "I mean, I shouldn't go with Kelly, and Slater shouldn't go with Jessie. It would be too distracting."

"Good idea, Zack," Jessie agreed crisply. "We have to keep our minds on the job. I'll watch with Lisa."

"And I'll watch with Screech," Zack said quickly.

Slater looked at the ground. Kelly looked at the sky.

"And you two can watch together," Zack told them. "Okay?"

"Sure," Slater said. It didn't take a genius to

see that Kelly didn't want to pair up with him. What had happened since they'd made their bargain at the pool? Could it be that she'd guessed his new feelings for her and was grossed out?

"Fine," Kelly said. She couldn't help feeling a little hurt that Slater didn't seem to want to stand watch with her.

"Come on, girls," Jessie said. "Let's go rustle up some blankets."

The girls hurried off toward their suite. Zack turned to Slater. "Thanks, buddy," he said fervently. "I am totally in your debt, man. There's this country and western jamboree at Tawnee's hotel. I have just enough time to slip away and meet her and her friends."

"You know, Kelly isn't a package you can just check when you're tired of carrying it," Slater burst out suddenly.

Zack looked at him, startled. "I know that. I love Kelly."

"Then why don't you start showing it?" Slater said. "One of these days, someone is going to come along who really appreciates her."

"I do appreciate her," Zack said. "Kelly knows that. I just got myself in this situation somehow. Come on, Slater. You can't tell me that if Tawnee was looking up at you and calling you a hero, that you'd just turn your back."

Yes, Slater wanted to say, *I would. Because Kelly is worth a hundred Tawnees.* But if he said it, Zack would know that he was developing a wicked crush on his girlfriend.

"Look, Slater, you're right, okay?" Zack said. He felt uncomfortable underneath Slater's stony gaze. He knew his friend was right, but he felt trapped in circumstances out of his control. It was fun being a completely different person for a few days. How could he pass up the opportunity to see what it was like to be a big rodeo star? And it wasn't as though he was cheating on Kelly. He hadn't kissed anybody or even held anybody's hand.

"It will all be over tomorrow," he said. "After tonight, I won't see the girls again. Okay, buddy?"

"Sure," Slater said. "It's your life, Zack."

"So you'll take care of Kelly?"

"I'll take care of her."

▲   ▼   ▲

Kelly and Slater settled down underneath a ponderosa pine tree near the far entrance of the stables. Slater spread a blanket on the soft pine needles and then wrapped another one around Kelly's shoulders.

"What about you, Slater?" Kelly asked.

"I'm not cold," he said. He leaned forward, his

hands dangling between his knees. He peered out into the darkness. Everything was quiet. The stars were like chips of cold ice strewn on black velvet. A quarter moon was tangled in the branches of a tree across the stable yard.

Next to him, he felt Kelly stir, and the scent of her perfume rose from her midnight hair. Slater gripped his hands together.

She's my best friend's girl.

Far away, in the mountains, an animal gave a sad, lonesome howl.

"What was that?" Kelly whispered.

"I'm not sure," Slater said. "Maybe a coyote. Don't worry, it was far away."

"I'm not scared," Kelly said, wrapping her arms around her knees. "I feel kind of stupid sitting here, actually. Do you really think Chance is going to drug one of the rodeo horses?"

"No," Slater said. "I don't."

"Me, neither," Kelly said with a soft giggle.

They were quiet for a minute. A horse stamped in his stall. Another horse blew out a long, snuffling breath.

"Listen, Slater," Kelly said in a small voice. "I know that the last thing you wanted was to pair off with me. If you want to watch with Jessie and Lisa, I'll be fine here. I'm not scared. Really."

"I'm not going to leave you here alone," Slater said gruffly.

So I was right, Kelly thought. *He didn't want to be alone with me.*

Even on their ride today, Slater had been different. Usually, it was so easy to be with him. He was always full of jokes and fun. But they'd hardly exchanged two words during the entire ride. Of course, they'd been riding single file on a trail, so it had been hard to talk. But Slater hadn't even made an effort.

A tear slowly welled up and slipped down Kelly's cheek. She knew it was silly to feel hurt. But she felt neglected by Zack, and now she felt rejected by Slater.

You're not making sense, Kelly, she scolded herself. Slater was probably just upset because he wasn't able to be alone with Jessie. Kelly wiped the tear away determinedly. She wasn't going to think about Slater that way. He was in love with Jessie.

Slater wasn't thinking about her at all. If he was thinking about her the way she was thinking about him, she'd know it. Because if he was, they'd probably be warming each other up this very minute instead of sitting here shivering. Suddenly Kelly wanted very, very much to know what it was like to kiss Slater.

"Kelly, maybe you should go inside," Slater said abruptly. "It's getting cold."

"I don't want to," Kelly said. "And you're the one who looks cold." She moved closer to Slater and slipped part of the blanket around his shoulders.

Pressed together with Slater under the blanket, Kelly felt her whole body get warmer. "This is much better," she said. "I guess I was pretty cold."

Slater licked his lips. He cleared his throat. Why did Kelly have to sit so close to him?

But she was close, and warm, and Zack was a jerk, and Jessie cared more about proving a point than being with him. Slater turned and finally looked at Kelly. Her skin glowed in the moonlight, and her blue eyes looked wide and expectant and very beautiful.

I can't, he thought.

I shouldn't, she thought.

But suddenly he leaned forward, and she leaned forward, and they were kissing.

▲ ▼ ▲

Lisa and Jessie sat back to back, each watching a separate entrance to the stable.

"Do you see anything?" Jessie whispered.

There was no answer.

Jessie poked Lisa with her elbow.

"Huh?" Lisa said, jerking upright.

"Stay awake!" Jessie ordered.

"Oh, Jessie, please let me sleep," Lisa pleaded. "When I go to sleep, I can forget how cold and uncomfortable I am. I keep dreaming about floating on an iceberg." Lisa shifted on the cold ground. "I can't believe how hard the ground is. It's impossible to get comfortable."

"You know, Lisa, people sleep on the ground all the time," Jessie said. "It's called camping."

Lisa shuddered. "Please. Don't mention that word when I'm around." She yawned. "Haven't we watched long enough?"

"Lisa, we have to protect the animals!" Jessie said. "Those poor horses."

"The horses are just fine," Lisa said. "They're probably sleeping, which is what every sensible person in Santa Fe is doing. You don't know for sure that Chance is going to do anything."

"I know," Jessie admitted reluctantly. She was cold and tired, too. "But what if he does, and we could have prevented it?"

Lisa yawned again. "I'd try to live with it."

Jessie sighed. Maybe she was being selfish, making all of her friends sit out here on the cold ground to wait for something that might not happen. They'd been out here for an hour, and Jessie's muscles felt frozen in the same position. If she sat out here any longer, Lisa would have to roll her down the path back to their suite.

Then Jessie thought about the bottle of horse tranquilizers she'd found. She'd already put it back in the stable medicine chest so that Chance wouldn't guess that someone was on to him. That was her biggest clue that something was going to happen, and probably tonight.

"But what about the bottle of tranquilizers I found?" she wondered aloud. "That's got to prove something."

"I've got an idea," Lisa said sleepily. "Why don't you go back and get it again? We can hide it or throw it away or something. Chance will just think he misplaced it. He'll never be able to get another bottle this late at night. So the rodeo horses will be safe for tomorrow."

"And meanwhile I'll come up with a plan to expose him tomorrow," Jessie said. "Lisa, you're a genius!"

"I know," Lisa said. "Now I would like to be a genius in my flannel pajamas, if you don't mind."

Jessie laughed and stood up. She reached down to help Lisa to her feet. "Come on. Let's go find Screech and Zack."

They walked to the next stable door and found Screech wrapped in blankets, fast asleep. Lisa poked him.

Screech's eyes flew open. "My dream came true!" he said, trying to stand up and reach for her. But the blankets were wrapped too tightly around him, and he fell back down.

"Down, boy," Lisa giggled.

"Where's Zack, Screech?" Jessie asked.

"Oh. He, uh, went back to the room," Screech said. "He had a, uh, stomachache."

"Oh," Jessie said. "I hope he's okay. You can go back and tell him not to worry. We're all going to go back to our rooms."

Screech tried to untangle himself from his blanket without success. Finally he just lay flat on the ground and unrolled himself. "Great. I'm ready to hit the hay. Well, not the hay. I'm tired of sleeping in a stable. I'll hit the mattress. Well, I won't hit the mattress, I'll just lie down on it—"

"Come on, Screech," Lisa said, taking his arm. "I think you're still asleep."

"I'll go find Slater and Kelly and tell them the good news," Jessie said. "Boy, I'll bet they'll be glad to see me!"

▲　▼　▲

Zack hopped off his bicycle as the Enchantment Lodge came into view, lit by luminaria all along its roofline. Luckily Tawnee's hotel was outside of town on the same road as the ranch. There was a bike path the whole way there.

He followed the sound of country and western music to a side entrance with a canopy reading CACTUS LOUNGE. A poster that hung on the door announced JAMBOREE TONIGHT! Zack pushed open the door and was met with warmth and color and the infectious sounds of a fiddle. Dancers were two-stepping on the dance floor. On a second tier, diners were watching the dancers below and clapping along.

Zack inched in, already smiling at the good spirits of the crowd. He saw Tawnee, Angel, and Crystal clapping along with the music at a small side table, and he went over to join them.

"Dave!" Tawnee's eyes lit up. "You're just in time."

"Isn't this great?" Angel said, tapping her foot to the beat.

"It looks like a really fun crowd," Zack said. "What am I just in time for? A dance?"

"Better than that," Tawnee said, standing up and grabbing his hand. "The mechanical bull riding competition is about to start. I signed you up for my team. I just know that you're a shoo-in to win!"

Chapter 10

▼　▲　▼　▲　▼

Jessie tramped across the dark stable yard. The moon was behind a cloud, and she had to be careful not to trip. Slater and Kelly were at the farthest end of the stable.

A tall ponderosa pine loomed ahead. Jessie squinted through the gloom and saw two pairs of feet sticking out from behind it. She didn't hear anything, though. The feet didn't move.

Some watchdogs! Jessie thought.

"Hey, you guys!" she called softly, walking toward the tree.

She heard a scuffling sound. As she rounded the trunk, Kelly popped up and looked at her, wild-eyed. Her hair was mussed, and she had a very guilty expression on her face. Slater wore the identical expression. His mouth dropped when he saw Jessie.

She put her hands on her hips. "Well, thanks a lot, you two. I know what you were doing!"

"Jessie, I can explain—," Kelly said.

"It—it just happened," Slater said.

"You were sleeping!" Jessie said, shaking a finger at them. "So much for keeping an eye out for criminals!"

Slater gulped. "Well . . . ," he said.

Kelly looked down. "Um . . . ," she said.

Jessie laughed. "Don't worry. I'm not mad. Lisa came up with a way to get us all warm and cozy. I took the tranquilizers out of the cabinet again. This way, hopefully Chance will think that he misplaced them. So he won't be able to do what he might have been planning to do. And we can all get some sleep!" She eyed Slater and Kelly. "You two look like you could use it."

Kelly brushed back her hair and began to fold the blanket. She didn't look at Slater. She couldn't look at Jessie. She was absolutely mortified! How could she have kissed Slater that way? She felt so guilty she didn't know if she could ever face Jessie again.

"Hurry up, you guys," Jessie urged. "You're moving like sleepwalkers. I have an idea how to get the truth about Chance tomorrow. I'll tell you about it on the way."

▲   ▼   ▲

"T-Tawnee, wait," Zack sputtered as Tawnee pulled him through the crowd.

But Tawnee was too excited to hear him. She had his hand firmly grasped in hers and she kept pulling. Zack saw that they were headed for a mechanical bull contraption that he'd only seen in the movies. In the movies, it had looked like a fun thing to do. But now it looked like an instrument of torture.

"Tawnee, wait," he said urgently as they came up to the crowd around the bull. "I can't—"

"Look, everybody!" Tawnee cried as she pushed through the circle and hauled Zack next to the bull. "Look who it is—Daredevil Dave Laramie!"

The crowd whooped and hollered. Zack tried to grin and gave a feeble wave. Why did Tawnee have to be so all-fired enthusiastic?

Tawnee clapped a hand on Zack's shoulder. "And he's on my team!" she cried.

"No," Zack said, but he was drowned out by the cheers of the crowd. They went wild, pounding the floorboards with their cowboy boots and whistling.

"All *right*, Dave!" someone shouted.

Zack was desperate. He pulled himself up on a

chair and held up a hand for quiet. After a moment and one last shrill whistle that nearly busted his eardrum, the crowd quieted.

"I can't ride tonight," Zack said. "For medical reasons. Got busted up by a bronc and the doc said no way, Davy."

A deep moan ran through the crowd. "Aw, Dave," someone said.

"But I will judge the competition," Zack offered.

Now the crowd cheered again. Zack could see Tawnee through the crowd. She was laughing up at him and shaking her head. Flaming highlights in her hair sparkled underneath the lights. She drew closer to him and grabbed the collar of his shirt.

"You deserve a dance, pardner," she murmured.

"What for?" Zack asked. He felt a little dazzled by the lights in his eyes.

Tawnee didn't reply. She only smiled as the announcer called out that the contest was about to start.

For the next hour, Zack had the best time of his life. He judged the contest amid much laughter and applause. He danced with Tawnee and Angel and Crystal. He told them more and more outlandish stories of his "career" as Daredevil Dave.

The girls egged him on, squealing with laughter at his jokes and gasping with horror at his near escapes. By the end of the evening, Zack was almost convinced that he really *was* Daredevil Dave Laramie!

The jamboree was still going strong when Zack looked at his watch and saw it was after midnight. He'd better get back before the gang gave up on watching the stables.

"Well, it's about that time, girls," he said. "I've got to be heading out."

Tawnee smiled at him. "I'm so glad you came, Dave. It was really fun."

"I had a fantastic time," Zack said. He really had. And now he felt a little guilty about deceiving the girls. They were so nice to him. Would they be as sweet to Zack Morris as they'd been to Daredevil Dave? Zack saw that there were drawbacks to pretending to be somebody else. What happened when the person you *became* was more fun than the person you *were*?

That was something Kelly might point out to him, Zack reflected. As usual, his girlfriend asked the right questions.

But it was late, and he didn't have time to think about it. If he didn't get back to the Lazybones Ranch, he wouldn't have a girlfriend to go back to.

Tawnee leaned toward him and touched his shoulder. "I'm glad you were able to dance with me, considering your hurt clavichord," she said.

Zack rubbed his arm. "Yeah, it's starting to twinge a mite, I have to admit."

"I thought you said it was your *left* clavichord," Angel pointed out, puzzled.

"Uh, it is," Zack said. "But it's connected to this nerve that runs all the way up to my shoulder and down my other arm. That's why it's so dangerous to strain it."

The girls nodded. "You're so brave," Tawnee said.

"I try," Zack said modestly. "Seeing the rodeo is really going to be hard, watching all my friends riding broncs. It'll kill me not to be able to wrassle and ride tomorrow."

He stood up. "Well, if you ladies will excuse me . . ."

Tawnee stood. "We'll walk you to the door, Dave."

Tawnee linked her slender arm through his as they walked to the door. "The rodeo is going to be real crowded tomorrow," she said. "So if I don't see you, Dave, I just want to say it was a real treat meeting you."

"It was a treat for me, too, Tawnee," Zack said sincerely.

"And if you're ever in Boulder, you look me up," she said. "Tawnee Jo Pride. Will you remember that?"

"I'll remember," Zack said.

When they were almost to the door, Zack heard a commotion over his head. He looked up.

On the second-floor tier, a waitress was carrying a large tray with a heavy glass pitcher on it. Zack watched as a big man tried to squeeze between her and the railing. The waitress's arm was jostled, and the tray began to tilt. As Zack watched in horror, the pitcher slid on the wet tray and was knocked off. It fell through the air to the floor below, straight toward Tawnee's head!

Zack didn't have time to think. He just dived forward and reached up at the same time. The pitcher fell into his hands as sweetly as a forward pass from Slater's powerful arm.

Tawnee gave a little scream. "Are you all right?" she asked Zack.

"I can't believe you caught that!" Angel said.

"Did you hurt yourself?" Crystal asked.

"I'm fine," Zack said. He handed the pitcher to another waitress as the folks around him burst into applause. Grinning, Zack took his last bow of the evening.

Tawnee's eyes were sparkling as she gripped Zack's arm to get his attention. "Did you see what just happened, girls?" she said. "Dave moved his left arm!"

The girls gasped. "And it worked perfectly!" Angel said.

"He raised it way over his head!" Crystal exclaimed.

"Do you know what this *means*?" Tawnee said excitedly.

"No," Zack said. "What?"

"Think about it, Dave. Your clavichord is completely healed," Tawnee said. "You can perform in the rodeo tomorrow!"

▲　▼　▲

The next morning, Jessie woke up early. She tiptoed out into the living room of the suite to the telephone. Flipping through a phone book, she punched out a number.

When the hotel clerk came on the line, she asked for Madge Moxley's room. In only two rings, the phone was picked up.

"Good morning," Madge said.

Jessie pinched her nose with her fingers. "Is this Madge Moxley speaking?"

"Sure is, honey. What can I do for you?"

"This is KSFS, the local radio station. We're happy to announce that you're the winner of a free ticket to today's rodeo out at the Lazybones Ranch!"

"Oh, my," Madge said. "I don't remember entering a contest or anything."

"Um, it was a random drawing of diners' names from the restaurant you ate in last night," Jessie improvised. "We like to thank our visitors for eating in our restaurants. Promotes tourism."

"But I had room service last night," Madge said.

"Oh, I meant Saturday night," Jessie said.

"Well, this is real nice," Madge said. "And I don't want to seem ungrateful. But I'm not what you'd call a big rodeo fan. So, thanks, anyw—"

"But you have to go!" Jessie broke in quickly. She pinched her nose again. "That is, ma'am, this is no ordinary rodeo. It's a once-in-a-lifetime experience you just can't miss."

"I can't?"

"You'll regret it, ma'am, for the rest of your life," Jessie said solemnly.

"Oh, dear, I can't decide. I haven't even had my coffee yet. I guess I'll just have to go then."

"Awesome!" Jessie exclaimed. "I mean, you've made an excellent decision, Mrs. Moxley. Your ticket will be waiting for you at the box office."

"What did you say your radio station was again, honey?"

Jessie scanned her memory banks and came up empty. "The local one," she said. "Have fun on us, Mrs. Moxley!"

She hung up the phone with a satisfied sigh. She'd done it. Once Chance came face-to-face with Madge Moxley in the bright sunshine today, her mom would have to admit that Jessie was right. Chance Gifford was Chuck MacGuffin, animal killer!

Chapter 11

▼　▲　▼　▲　▼

Lisa was still blow-drying her hair, so Jessie suggested that she and Kelly walk over to the main lodge for breakfast together. The last thing Kelly wanted to do was be alone with Jessie, but what could she do?

They strolled underneath the pine trees. Kelly took deep gulps of the fresh morning air, hoping it would dispel the cloud of guilt around her head.

"You might not believe this, but I'm looking forward to getting back to Palisades," Jessie remarked as they walked.

"You are?" Kelly asked. "It's so beautiful here, though."

"I know," Jessie said. "But I haven't had a chance to enjoy it. I'm spending too much time worrying about my mom. I can tell that Slater isn't crazy about it, too." She sighed. "I really wanted this weekend to bring us closer together, but we seem farther apart."

"Well, you have been running around a lot, trying to get the goods on Chance," Kelly said.

"And Slater just doesn't understand," Jessie said, breaking off some pine needles and crushing them for the fresh scent. "Sometimes he's so stubborn. But I know that things will be better when we get back to Palisades."

"I'm sure they will," Kelly said faintly.

"I'll make it up to him," Jessie said. "I'll go to some of his wrestling matches. I'll even try to surf with him."

"I don't think Slater wants you to do what he likes because you feel you have to," Kelly said.

Jessie shrugged. "I know. But I will, anyway. I don't like wrestling, but I love Slater."

"You really do, don't you, Jessie," Kelly said quietly.

"Well, sure," Jessie said as they reached the lodge. "Just the way you love Zack."

▲   ▼   ▲

Zack drew the curtains and sighed. He'd been hoping for a steady downpour or maybe a blizzard. A typhoon, a monsoon, even a Santa Ana wind. But the day was bright and clear. The rodeo would take place as scheduled.

There was only one thing to do: be a man. Fake a stomachache.

The girls were coming to the rodeo today, and they just couldn't see him. Zack would have to stay in the suite all day. But he'd have to tell someone why. Because he'd gotten in so late, he'd overslept. Screech and Slater were already gone, and when he'd called the girls' suite, there was no answer.

Zack looked at his watch. He had just enough time to find Kelly and the gang and fake a stomachache before the rodeo started. He'd blame it on all those hot chili peppers. Then he could safely hide in his room for the day. He'd miss the rodeo, but maybe Jessie was right. Maybe it was just a macho sport that endangered animals so that men could feel like cowboys.

He dressed quickly and hurried over to the main house. The man at the front desk told him that his friends had already eaten breakfast and had gone over to watch the rodeo setting up. Zack left and headed for the rodeo grounds near the stables.

He found Screech petting a calf near the stable door. He was dressed in his vest, chaps, and cowboy hat.

"Hey, Screech," Zack said. "Have you seen Kelly?"

Screech frowned as he tipped his hat back. "I reckon the little filly is with Slater. Those two cowpokes seem to be spending a heap of time together."

"I'll look for them," Zack said. "Catch you later, Screech."

"That's pardner to you," Screech called after him.

Zack walked off and headed for the stands. There was a split-rail fence separating him from the large area where the rodeo was setting up. Zack reached up to haul himself over it.

But he stopped when he heard a terrible, scary sound. It was the sound of a name being called. It wasn't *his* name. It was a name he never wanted to hear again.

"Daredevil Dave!"

Zack turned around slowly. Tawnee, Crystal, and Angel were heading toward him. He groaned under his breath. These girls were persistent.

"Hi!" Tawnee called as she came up. "We came out early. We were hoping we'd see you before it got too crowded."

"Hi," Zack said weakly.

"I guess your clavichord is still okay," Angel observed. "We saw you climbing the fence."

Zack nodded. "Listen, it's great to see you girls. But I was just on my way to check something."

"Wait," Angel said. "We have something for you." She reached behind her and held up a pair of chaps. "We saw that skinny manager of yours wearing these, and we asked if we could borrow them. You said you didn't have any of your rodeo gear here in Santa Fe."

Thanks, Screech! Zack took the chaps gingerly. "Gee. I don't know what to say. Well, I'd better get going."

"We'll come with you," Tawnee said. "We already talked to one of the hands, and he said it wouldn't be against the rules for us to pick out the bronco for you to ride. Won't that be fun?"

"Pick out the bronc—"

But the girls were already hustling him toward the animals, each in separate pens. They walked along, looking carefully at each horse. Then, in the last pen, Zack saw a massive black head looming above the divider. One wild eye rolled. A hoof smashed behind into the boards, and they splintered.

Oh, no, Zack thought. *Not that one. Not that—*

"That's the one!" Tawnee sang out.

"Uh, wait a second, girls," Zack said. "I'm not sure my clavichord—"

"Yoo-hoo!" Crystal sang out to a nearby rodeo worker. "Can you put this one down for this guy here to ride?"

"You bet," the worker said. "You're the only one who wants to ride Lightning."

"After that, we can pick out a cow for you to wrassle," Tawnee said happily.

Zack stumbled backward dizzily as Lightning kicked the stall. How was he going to do this? The only experience he'd ever had with horses was riding a docile old mare who'd thought trotting was a huge effort!

▲   ▼   ▲

Jessie waited eagerly by the front gate. She peered through the branches of a tree as person after person gave his or her ticket to the attendant. She was beginning to think that Madge had said she'd show up just to be polite. But then she saw Madge pause at the ticket stand. She was wearing a wide-brimmed straw hat and yet another sweat-shirt.

Jessie heaved a sigh of relief as the attendant handed her the ticket Jessie had bought earlier that morning. Madge was smiling as she walked through the gate.

Jessie hurried toward her. "Mrs. Moxley, hi!"

Madge waved. "Hey, Jessie!"

"You remember my name," Jessie said.

"I never forget a face," Madge said.

Boy, I hope that's true, Jessie thought. "So do

you like rodeos?" Jessie asked, falling into step beside Madge.

"Not particularly," Madge admitted. "I won a ticket in some kind of contest I never entered from a radio station I never heard of." She gave a hoot of laughter. "I tried to call them back, but the local station said they weren't running any contest. I must have gotten the station wrong or something."

"Probably," Jessie said, her cheeks flaming. "All radio stations run contests."

"Well, I guess I was meant to be here, so here I am," Madge said. "I'm leaving for home tomorrow, so I figure that this is a good way to end my visit to the Wild West."

Jessie was subtly guiding Madge toward the section of the bleachers where Chance and her mother had staked out seats. She had to distract Madge, though, in case the woman decided she wanted to go and pet calves or get a lemonade.

"So have you been enjoying your stay in Santa Fe?" Jessie asked. "How have you liked the Hilton?"

Madge gave her a curious look. "You know where I'm staying?"

"Well," Jessie said confusedly, "you mentioned it last time. I never forget a face, either," she said. "Or a hotel."

"I like the hotel just fine," Madge said. "It's

beautiful. Not as nice as this place, though. Next time, I'd like to stay outside of town on a ranch like this."

Jessie seized on this as her opening. "Would you like to meet the owner? I could introduce you."

"Really? That would be real nice," Madge said.

Bingo! Jessie took Madge's arm and led her toward the south end of the bleachers. She could see Chance's tall form standing next to them, her mother beside him. They were talking to a group of Chance's friends. As Jessie approached, the men and women around Chance let out a shout of laughter as he made a remark.

Chance chuckled along with them, his face creased in a genial grin. But the grin slowly faded as Jessie and Madge walked up.

Beside her, she heard Madge gasp.

Chance looked stricken.

I knew it! Jessie thought. "Chance," she said, bringing Madge forward, "I want you to meet a new friend of mine. This is Madge Moxley. Madge, this is Chance Gifford."

"I'm pleased to meet you," Chance said. His voice was low and steady. Jessie saw her mother give him a quick, puzzled look. His friends quieted and looked from Madge to Chance. They sensed something strange was going on.

"Madge is from Virginia," Jessie said.

Chance nodded. His eyes didn't drop from Madge's face. They stood, staring at each other.

"Madge, are you all right?" Jessie asked. "You look like you've seen a ghost."

Jessie's mom looked at her. "Jessie—," she said warningly.

"Do you know Chance, Madge?" Jessie prompted. "You said he looked familiar." She waited confidently for the answer.

There was a long pause. Then Madge turned to her. "He looks like someone I used to know. But now that I get up close, I can see that it's not the same man at all."

Madge smiled pleasantly. "It's nice to meet you, Mr. Gifford. You've got a beautiful spread here."

"Thank you, Madge," Chance said gravely. "Thank you very much."

Madge turned away. Ignoring her mother's angry look, Jessie hurried after Madge. She caught up to her by the split-rail fence.

"Madge, wait!" Jessie said.

Madge turned around, and Jessie saw she was angry, too. "I think I'm beginning to see the light," she said. "You sent me that ticket, didn't you?"

Jessie nodded shamefacedly. "I had to," she said. "I had to see you face-to-face with him."

"Who is he to you?" Madge asked.

"He's my mother's boyfriend," Jessie explained. "I just don't want her to get hurt, Madge. Can you understand that?" she said pleadingly.

The anger left Madge's face. "Sure, hon," she said.

"Madge, you didn't tell the truth back there," Jessie said. "I know you didn't. Can't you go back with me now?"

Madge tilted her head and looked at her kindly. "Jessie, Chuck MacGuffin was a friend of mine. If that man was him, I'd treat him as a friend. If he didn't want to be found, I'd leave him in peace."

Jessie stared at her, confused. "But—"

Madge patted her arm. "Now I think I'll head back to town. I prefer to see my horses trotting around a pasture. Good-bye, Jessie."

Jessie watched Madge walk away. She'd lost her opportunity to expose Chance. She couldn't force Madge to recognize him. Now her mother would never believe her.

She turned away, disappointed. But her troubles weren't over. Chance and her mother were pushing through the crowd, heading her way. And they didn't look happy at all.

Chapter 12

▼　▲　▼　▲　▼

Jessie threw her shoulders back and faced them defiantly. She wasn't going to let Chance Gifford, or even arch-criminal Chuck MacGuffin, push her around!

"Jessie, just tell me one thing," her mother said when they reached her. "Did you invite that woman here to embarrass Chance?"

"Yes, I did," Jessie said boldly. "Why shouldn't he be embarrassed? Even though Madge wouldn't admit it, he's an imposter and a . . . a criminal on the lam!"

"Jessie, listen to me—," her mother began.

"No, you listen for once, Mom!" Jessie said. "You wouldn't listen to me the other night. But I've checked up on Chance. That's not his real name.

He committed a crime in Virginia eight years ago. He poisoned a horse, Mom! Just to win a race. And he was planning to do the same thing again, right here!"

Chance frowned. "Here? What are you talking about, Jessie?"

"I found your horse tranquilizers, Chance, or Chuck, or whatever your name is," Jessie flung at him.

"So?" Chance said. "Every ranch probably has a bottle of old horse tranquilizers around. Horses get sick."

"But these weren't *old*," Jessie said craftily. "The prescription was dated last week. And I asked the stable hands, and they said that none of the horses were sick!" she finished, tossing her head.

"Jessie, enough of this," her mother snapped.

Chance put a hand on her mother's arm. "It's okay, Kate." He turned to Jessie. "Last week, Rebel, one of the horses, hurt her leg on the trail. The vet wrote out a prescription just in case she wasn't available if the swelling got worse. It never did. Rebel is just fine."

Jessie stared at him stonily. "Why should I believe you?" she said.

"No reason why you should," Chance answered. "But you can call the vet yourself, if you'd like. Her name is Dr. Lucinda Beringer. She's in the book."

"Well, maybe you can explain away the tran- quilizers," Jessie said. "But you can't explain away changing your name and running away from crimi- nal charges in Virginia."

"Criminal charges?" Chance asked.

"Well, they were almost filed against you. You were suspected of conspiring to drug a horse just to win a race. And the horse died! Then you ran away. You're just a low-down criminal, and you're trying to take advantage of my mom!" Jessie turned to Mrs. Spano. "Mom, you've got to believe me!"

"I do believe you, Jessie," her mom said.

"Thank goodness," Jessie breathed.

"I knew it all already," her mom said, with a quick glance at Chance. "Chance told me every- thing before he brought us out here this weekend."

Stunned, Jessie leaned back against the fence. "He . . . what?"

"And if you give him a chance to talk, he'll explain everything to you, too," her mother said.

"Will you listen, Jessie?" Chance asked.

"Please, Jess," her mother said.

Jessie nodded slowly. "Okay."

"I *am* Chuck MacGuffin," Chance said. "Chance was a nickname my father had for me when I was a kid. He always caught me playing poker in the stables. And Gifford is my middle name. I had to change my name when I left Virginia."

"So you did have to leave," Jessie said.

Chance nodded. "But I didn't drug that horse, Jessie. My horse farm was in financial trouble. I was close to losing it, and everybody in the county knew it. Then I was approached by a man who said he knew a way for me to keep the farm. It didn't take me long to figure out what he was talking about. But he brought in the rest of his cronies and tried to pressure me. It turned out they made a practice of infiltrating horse breeders all across the world. They'd find out who needed money and move in, getting the owners to drug their horses in order to fix races."

"That's awful," Jessie said.

Chance nodded. "I refused to have anything to do with them. The night before a race a bunch of them broke into my stables and drugged my horse without my knowing. I ran the horse in the race and he died. They were hoping to frame me, but luckily the authorities believed my story. I gave them information on the gang, and they were able to catch the ringleader. But the rest escaped, and they threatened me. The authorities thought it would be a good idea for me to leave town. Considering that my business was failing and someone was trying to kill me, I thought it would be a good idea, too. I sold the farm to a neighbor on a handshake and left. I changed my name, just in case they were persistent. That's why I'm here."

Jessie was quiet as she tried to absorb Chance's story. She had to admit it all made sense.

"You see, Jessie?" her mother prompted.

Jessie nodded slowly. "I guess I flew off the handle," she said. "I'm really sorry, Chance. I could learn a lesson from Madge. She knew how to be a true friend to you."

"Jessie, it's okay," Chance said. "You knew something was fishy, and you followed up on it. I admire that. And I want you to know something. The reason I don't want anyone to know my real name now is basically just to be cautious. I've been safe out here for years, but now I have to think about your mom. I would never put her or you in any danger. If those guys are still looking for me, they're looking in horse-racing circles for a guy named MacGuffin." He put an arm around Mrs. Spano. "I love your mom, you know."

"I know," Jessie said. Now that she knew the real story, she realized that she *did* like Chance.

Maybe that had been the problem, Jessie realized, catching her breath. Maybe she hadn't wanted to like Chance. Because if she liked him too much and he left, she'd miss him. Just like she missed her dad.

"I'm really sorry, Mom," she blurted. "I acted like a real jerk. I never listen to anybody, do I? And I never learn."

Mrs. Spano reached over and hugged Jessie. "I wouldn't change you for anything, Jess. You follow your heart. There's nothing wrong with that. But maybe, just once in a while, you could try to trust other people the way you trust your instincts. You have to have a little faith in people."

"You're right, Mom," Jessie said. "Slater tells me that, too. I'll try to remember it."

Chance linked an arm through Jessie's. "What do you say we go enjoy the rodeo? I hear the music. It must be starting up."

"Come on, sweetie," Mrs. Spano said. "We saved you and the gang seats."

Jessie felt as though a weight had been lifted from her shoulders as she headed to the stands with her mom and Chance. She couldn't wait to see Slater. She couldn't wait to tell him he'd been right. She had gone off half-cocked, and she'd spoiled his vacation. But she knew Slater would forgive her. He always did.

▲   ▼   ▲

"Kelly!"

Kelly heard Slater, but she pretended not to. She didn't turn. She just kept walking.

"Kelly!"

She ducked behind a lemonade stand and waited, her heart pounding. But a second later, a curly head of hair popped around the corner.

"Why are you running away from me?" Slater demanded.

"I'm not running away," Kelly said. "I was . . . thirsty."

He reached over and grabbed her hand. "Come with me."

Kelly hung back. "Why?"

Slater's face was grim. "Because we have to talk."

Together they climbed all the way to the top of the stands. Surrounded by the crowd, they could be alone. Slater kept Kelly's hand in his as they climbed, but he dropped it when they sat down.

"Why are you avoiding me, Kelly?" he asked quietly. "You walked out of the dining room as soon as I came in this morning. You didn't even finish your breakfast. And you've been running around the rodeo so much, I'm dizzy from trying to keep up with you."

"I'm not—," Kelly started, but she sighed. "I am," she admitted. "I guess I was afraid to see you, Slater. After—"

"After last night," Slater finished. "Do you regret it?"

Kelly peeked at him under her bangs. "Do you?"

He grinned. "Are you kidding? Not for one single second."

Kelly let out the breath she'd been holding. "Me, neither," she admitted. "I feel guilty, no question. But I don't regret it."

"As a matter of fact, it was the best time I've had in a long, long time," Slater said.

"I feel the same way," Kelly said in a rush.

"Look, Kelly," Slater said. "Jessie was my first love. I'll always care for her. But I think it's time that we both moved on. We're just too different to take it any farther."

Kelly nodded. "And I've been starting to think about me and Zack. It's so *hard* to love him. He'll never stop scamming and scheming and getting himself in impossible situations. It's not that I want him to change. But it's easier to deal with him as his friend than his girlfriend. I can take a step back when we're not going out. I can just laugh along with the rest of you guys and say, well, that's Zack for you. But as his girlfriend, I have to worry all the time. Not to mention get hurt."

Slater nodded. "He's a handful. So is Jessie." He turned to face her. "That's what I like about *us*, Kelly. I like being with you. We like the same things. We have fun together. It feels more . . .

equal with you. Jessie is always running things, and I feel like I'm always trying to catch up."

Kelly nodded. "I know what you mean."

"I just want to sit and relax with someone sometimes," Slater said.

"So do I," Kelly said.

Slater reached over and took her hand. "Last night . . . well, it was incredible. To be with you, under the stars."

"I know," Kelly said. "It was incredible." She'd never thought that kissing someone other than Zack could be so wonderful. But it had been.

"So what are we going to do about us?" Slater asked.

"Is there an *us*, Slater?" Kelly asked.

He played with her fingers. "I don't know. There could be. I want there to be. Do you?"

"I don't know," Kelly said. "I'm really not sure, Slater. I mean, I don't want to hurt Jessie."

Slater nodded. "I don't, either. That's why I'm going to break it off when we get back to Palisades."

"Are you sure you want to do that?"

Slater nodded. "I'm sure. Look, Kelly, I'm not going to pressure you. Things are over between me and Jessie. I love her, but I just can't be with her anymore. So I'll be around. When you're ready, I'll be there."

Kelly squeezed his fingers. "I don't know what to say." She looked at him, her heart in her eyes. She really liked him. But could she break things off with Zack?

He grinned. "Don't say anything. Just keep looking at me that way."

He leaned over and kissed her. Kelly kissed him back. But she felt guilty, and they broke apart quickly.

"Gosh, Slater," Kelly said. "Maybe it would be better to just tell Zack and Jessie what happened. I hate sneaking around like this."

"I know," Slater said. "I'm not sure what's the right thing to do."

Just then Screech pounded up the bleachers toward them. Slater quickly dropped Kelly's hand.

"I've been looking everywhere for you guys," Screech said, panting. "You have to come with me."

"What is it, Screech?" Kelly asked in alarm.

"Zack is about to kill himself!" Screech announced.

Kelly and Slater exchanged a worried glance. Had Zack heard about them already? Because of them, was he going to end it all?

Chapter 13

▼ ▲ ▼ ▲ ▼

He had no choice. He had to do it. He had to ride the bronco. If he told the girls that he wasn't Daredevil Dave, he'd be dead meat. And if he refused to ride, he'd be a wimp.

So instead, Zack told himself, *you'll be a dead wimp.*

He hoped his shaking legs weren't apparent to the girls. He could hear the roar of the crowd from the bleachers. He could smell the scent of macho, sweat, and horses. He could do it, he told himself. Wasn't he excellent on a skateboard, a killer on a bicycle, super daring on Rollerblades? He had balance and nerve and strong ankles. What else could he need?

"Hey, Joe!" a rodeo hand called. "You'd better

bring the ambulance closer. This one's riding Lightning!"

Zack took a shaky step backward and bumped into Tawnee. "Oh, Dave," she said. "This is so thrilling! Aren't you excited?"

"You bet," Zack croaked. "I'm about to pass out."

The rodeo hand signaled to Zack. "You're up, fella."

"It's funny that he doesn't know you," Tawnee whispered. "Shouldn't you tell him you're Daredevil Dave so that they can announce it over the loudspeaker?"

"I've been off the circuit for a while, Tawnee," Zack replied. "I'd rather stay incognito for this one. Okay?"

"Okay." Tawnee clapped him on the back. "Good luck, Dave."

"We'll be rooting for you," Angel said.

"And don't worry," Crystal assured him. "The ambulance is real close by."

Zack swallowed. He tried to smile. "Great."

The rodeo cowboy motioned him forward to the pen where Lightning waited. Zack had been watching the other performers, so he knew what to do. He put one foot on the gate on one side of the animal and one foot on the other. Now he was poised over Lightning's back. When he gave the signal, he would drop onto the back of the bronco; the cowboy would open the latch at the same time. After that, it was a battle between man and beast. Looking at Lightning snort angrily, Zack knew who would win.

Would Kelly still love him in traction? he wondered. It might cut into his dancing skills at the prom.

"Get ready," the cowboy said as he squinted at the field where a cowboy was desperately trying to stay on a bucking bronco. "This guy isn't going to last long."

A deafening roar broke out from the crowd.

"It's over," the cowboy said. "I'll count down from ten. On *one*, give the signal that you're going to drop onto Lightning and I'll lift the latch. Ten, nine,—"

Tawnee peered into the ring and came back to Zack. "The last guy did pretty good. Only a small compound fracture."

"A c-compound f-fracture?"

"Seven, six—get set," the cowboy warned.

"Oh, Dave," Tawnee said meltingly. "I'll be here waiting."

"We'll ride with you in the ambulance," Crystal said.

"Five, four—" the cowboy continued. His hand reached for the latch.

Sweat slipped down Zack's forehead and slid into his eyes. It stung. He couldn't even see. How was he going to stay on for more than a fraction of a second? Lightning would probably throw him right into the bleachers.

"Three—" the cowboy said.

Zack lifted his hand to give the signal. This was it. He was about to be broken into a million different pieces. If he did have a clavichord somewhere, it would be pulverized.

"Two—"

Zack closed his eyes.

"That's enough, Mac," Tawnee said. There was laughter in her voice.

Zack opened his eyes. Mac, the rodeo worker, was grinning. Crystal had her hand over her mouth, trying to smother her laughter. Angel was leaning on her helplessly as she laughed silently.

Tawnee grinned at him. *"Gotcha!"*

"Wh-what happened?" Zack asked dazedly.

Mac the cowboy grinned. "You can get off now, fella. Be careful not to kick Lightning."

Zack gingerly climbed back over the fence. He swung over the gate and landed with a thump in front of Tawnee.

"I'll say this much for you," she said, her eyes shining from tears of laughter. "You've got guts. You were about to go out there, weren't you?"

"I think so," Zack said.

"You could have been killed," Crystal said, shaking her head. "You must be nuts."

"I've heard that before," Zack said. "So I guess you know I'm not Daredevil Dave Laramie, huh?"

Tawnee, Crystal, and Angel nodded.

"A busted clavichord?" Tawnee scoffed. "You've got to be kidding. Never try to fool a premed student."

"We knew something was wrong at lunch that day," Crystal explained. "Then we saw you with your friends later and figured out that you definitely weren't Dave."

"So why did you let me go on like that?" Zack asked, brushing the dust off his pants.

"We don't like being fooled," Tawnee said. "It doesn't feel very good, does it?"

"No," Zack admitted. "It doesn't. But Tawnee, Crystal, Angel—I wasn't doing it to be mean. I just . . . enjoyed the attention, I guess. What guy would turn down being worshiped by three beautiful girls?"

Tawnee laughed. "You're still a charmer. What's your real name, anyway?"

"Zack Morris," Zack said. "I'm from California."

"Well, Zack Morris, it's nice to meet you at last," Tawnee said, reaching out to shake his hand.

"Thanks for making our trip to Santa Fe so memorable. We had fun turning the tables on you. I tried to do it at the jamboree, but you got out of riding the mechanical bull. That's when Crystal decided that we should use a real animal."

"Gee, thanks, Crystal," Zack said.

"You're lucky," Crystal said. "It was Tawnee who said we shouldn't let you get into the ring. She just wanted to scare you."

"Just wanted to prove a point," Tawnee added.

"Well, you did a very good job," Zack said. "I'll let you know when I stop shaking."

The girls laughed and turned away.

"Hold on a sec," Zack said. "Where are you going?"

"We've got a plane to catch," Tawnee said. "But remember how I told you to look me up if you were ever in Boulder?"

Zack brightened. "You bet."

Tawnee grinned cheerfully. "I lied. Have a nice life, Zack."

Zack's jaw dropped as he watched the girls walk away. He guessed he'd deserved that. Maybe it had been kind of a lousy trick to play on the girls. He just hadn't been thinking clearly. Once he'd started the scam, it had just kept rolling forward. Wasn't Kelly always telling him to stop and think?

Kelly. At least Zack had one consolation: Kelly

didn't know about his bonehead ruse with the girls. At least he'd lucked out in that area.

Just then he caught sight of Kelly hurrying toward him with Slater and Screech.

"Zack, are you okay?" Kelly asked anxiously. "Screech said that you were about to kill yourself. I know he exaggerates, but—"

Zack threw a warning glance at Screech. "I'm fine, Kelly. I had a stomachache before. Maybe I ate one too many chili peppers. But I feel better now. Why don't we find our seats?"

"Mrs. Spano saved us some over there," Slater said.

The four of them found Lisa and Jessie already there, waiting for them. "Hurry up," Lisa called. "You're missing all the fun."

Jessie patted the seat next to her, and Slater slid into it. "I have so much to tell you," she whispered. "Everything's okay with Chance now."

"So you were wrong about him?" Slater asked.

"No," Jessie said. "I wasn't wrong. But I wasn't right, either. I'll tell you after the rodeo."

Zack sat down with Kelly. It felt good to be with his girl, even though it was their last day in Santa Fe. He intended to make the most of it. Thank goodness she didn't realize what he'd been up to.

Kelly scanned her program. "Hey, I don't see

your name here," she said to Zack. Her blue eyes twinkled. "Aren't you performing today, *Daredevil Dave?*"

Zack gulped. "You *knew?*"

Kelly nodded. "I knew."

"Gosh," Zack said ruefully. "This is scary. Everyone was on to me the whole time. I really must be losing my touch."

Jessie leaned over. "Or maybe girls aren't as gullible as you think."

"Oh, well," Zack said. "At least you're not too mad at me, Kelly. And everything is back to normal."

"I thought you didn't *like* normal, remember?" Kelly pointed out.

"I'm beginning to appreciate its virtues," Zack said.

"That's right," Jessie agreed. "Finally we can relax and enjoy ourselves. Everything's just the way it should be."

She smiled and snuggled closer to Slater. Zack grinned and put his arm around Kelly's shoulders. Both Zack and Jessie missed the look that passed between Slater and Kelly.

Yes, Zack and Jessie thought, *everything's back to normal at last . . .*

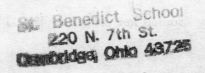
St. Benedict School
220 N. 7th St.
Cambridge, Ohio 43725